THE BARON TO BREAK

ALL THAT GLITTERS

TAMMY ANDRESEN

THE BARON TO BREAK

What if Prince Charming wasn't so charming? What if he was the bad guy?

Baron Robinson liked it that way. Except when his best friend's sister, the lovely Miss Emily Cranston, is suddenly alone in the world, he knows it's his duty to protect her.

Keeping her safe turns out to be a much larger job than he anticipated. Because while Emily is the picture of innocence, the trouble nipping at her heels is anything but.

Jacob might be a no-good rake…but a lady that vulnerable needs to be protected from real evil.

And the fact that she tempts him in all sorts of ways she ought not…. Well, he's just going to have to keep her safe from that too. But while saving her from the world is a challenge, keeping his hands off her is proving to be impossible.

NOTE TO READER

This story is a twisted retelling of "Sleeping Beauty." As I dug into the various versions of this fairy tale, some elements were best left in the dark ages (they creeped me out) while others were great elements to plant in this story. For example, in some versions, the prince was already married, which was not for us, while in others, the hero has a mother who attempts to kill Sleeping Beauty after they are wed! Disney left that part out, but I thought it would be great for our story. This might be the loosest of all the fairy tales in the "All That Glitters" series. I wanted Jacob to be her reluctant brother's best friend which is not part of the any version of the original fairy tale, but Emily is definitely waking from a long sleep and finally learning to face her life. I hope you enjoy!

PROLOGUE

JACOB HATED FUNERALS. No one liked them, he was certain of that, but somehow, all that was wrong with his world had coalesced into one single event the day he'd buried his father and become Baron Robinson.

Not that he hadn't known that his mother was part of why his particular world was so awful. But she'd stood next to his father's grave, her elaborately designed dress stitched with layer upon layer of the finest lace dyed black, staring down at the grave with a marked frown. She'd not cried, nor had she said a single word of comfort to him.

She did hold the hand of his younger brother who'd stared sight-lessly at the grave below. Eric wasn't a bad brother as brothers went, but their mother did everything in her power to pit them against each other. Like now, holding Eric's hand and not his.

On his other side had stood his best friend and the most steadying force in the world, Ashton Cranston.

Jacob drew in a deep breath, Ashton giving him a near impercep-tible nod of comfort. Which was the only reason he managed to keep a blank stare when his mother had turned to him, the dirt not even covering his father's grave, as she'd softly hissed, "I expect you to uphold your father's treatment of me."

He knew what she meant. Money. Always money with her. "Whatever do you mean, Mother? Could you be referring to the level of affection the two of you clearly shared?" His mother made no bones about the fact that she despised her husband. They'd been matched by their families. Poorly.

His mother, who wished to spend money without any limits, despised that her husband did the same. His mother was right in this one regard. Jacob's father had been awful at running the finances. A fact that Jacob was going to have to right. His stomach clenched with dread knowing the uphill battle he faced.

"You know very well that I am used to a certain standard of living," she hissed, ignoring the other guests that went by. She wasn't foolish enough to be overheard but she didn't grace them with even a nod either. It was always all about her.

"You'll have to learn to live differently, Mother. Now that Father is dead, his debts are being called in. There is no choice." Jacob glanced over at his friend so see Ashton softly greeting guests on their behalf as Jacob conducted this lovely little back and forth with his mother.

She'd sneered. "This wouldn't be happening if Eric were the heir."

Ashton's hand gave him the slightest tap on the shoulder. Jacob knew his best friend was silently comforting him and from his position could hear every word, unlike the rest of the guests.

"I fail to see how Eric would have stopped our father from becoming indebted."

"He'd take care of me," she pushed out through clenched teeth. At five and thirty, his mother was still a great beauty, with flawless skin and large green eyes. Eyes that he shared. He briefly wondered what other parts of her lived inside him.

"Of course he would. And so will I," he murmured, staring back at the coffin.

"Don't listen," Ash had whispered, having stepped closer to Jacob's side. "She's too selfish to see what a good man you are."

"Thank you," he whispered back. "I think I'm going to need a glass of whiskey after this." Maybe the entire bottle. Anything to numb the loss of his father and the nagging doubt his mother didn't care a lick about him.

What else might drown the pain pulsing through his chest?

———

TEN YEARS LATER, he stood at a second funeral, no more comfortable than he'd been on the day he'd buried his father.

First, standing over another grave reminded him of all the choices he'd made during the last decade.

Financially, he'd made progress. Personally, however...

Jacob stood on the outskirts of a different funeral. Now it was Ash's turn to bury not just one parent but both of his parents.

And despite the fact they'd drifted apart over the past ten years, Jacob living on the outskirts of society as he worked through his father's debt and Ashton in the middle of the *ton*, Ash continued to be kind and helpful. He'd even aided Jacob in a few business ventures that had done a great deal to reduce the heavy burden Jacob carried.

Which was why he'd come today. Ash still deserved his allegiance and his support.

But something was very wrong because Ash wasn't here today. He was not attending his parents' funeral. Unlike Jacob's family, Ash loved his parents and his sister, and he'd take great pains to see them cared for.

Where was his friend?

Ashton's sister, Emily Cranston, stood alone over the two graves. He was struck first by her straight, dignified posture, and next by the tears that, despite the black veil that covered her eyes, still appeared on her cheeks and chin. Her lips quivered as she took several notice-able gulps.

He watched guests file past her, he noted the way, even through the grief, she held their hands, kissed their cheeks, thanked them for their support, offered them comfort.

He'd never seen a woman so young act with such kindness and

grace. She stole his breath with how warmly dignified she looked there while standing all alone.

After a decade, he'd still not cleared his father's debt entirely, and his relationship with his mother was more contentious then ever. He had enough problems still to sink a man.

But Ash had been the only thing that had held him up that day and as he watched Emily today, he knew someone had to do the same for her.

Ash deserved his help.

And as he watched Emily, he knew without a doubt, she deserved it too.

CHAPTER ONE

THERE ARE times in life where change is so slow, it seems as though it isn't happening at all. Miss Emily Cranston, daughter of Viscount and Viscountess Marsden, had spent years hoping to be out from beneath her mother's watchful eye.

And for years, absolutely nothing had changed in this regard. Emily's mother decided which parties she attended, to whom she spoke, what she ate, and when she slept. Emily had secretly begged for the iron hand of her mother to be lifted so that she might choose something, anything, for herself.

But now, at the age of twenty, without warning, not even the smallest hint, the greatest change of them all had occurred. Death.

Didn't people often have a premonition in this regard? Some clue, a shiver or a dream or *something* that warned them irrevocable circumstances were about to occur?

She'd received not even the smallest hint...

And in one swift accident, a muddy road and an overturned carriage, she'd lost both her parents, and now, Emily found herself alone. She was finally able to make her own decisions, and she'd give it all back to have her parents with her. Alive. A tear slid down her cheek, covered by the veil she still wore on her head.

The funeral had been hours ago, but she'd not bothered to take her heavy veil off, nor had she removed the simple black gloves that still covered her hands. Anything lavish would have seemed...wrong.

Her brother had been gone for near a year on some tour of Europe and while word had been sent to him, Emily had no idea when he might return or how long she'd have to drift along these halls without a bit of company. He'd been due back months ago and not only had he not come home, they'd not received a single letter since he'd left France bound for Spain. Worry fluttered in her stomach.

She felt like a ghost in this moment, alone and not really living at all.

No one had prepared her for such an event. She'd been smothered in attention for years. What would she even do alone?

Her mother had been attempting to match Emily with some suitable lord for the last year and a half. Emily had tried her utmost to avoid the matches, not having found any of the men of particular interest.

They'd been much older, or dull, or not particularly handsome. Her mother had regularly thrown up her hands. "Lord Tinderwell owns more land than any duke in England. What's the matter with you?"

"The matter?" she'd ask. Lord Tinderwell was twice her age and not a particularly good conversationalist. Was it wrong for a girl to wish for a bit of adventure? Excitement? Romance even?

She winced as she blotted more tears from her eyes. If she'd listened to her mother, she wouldn't be in this predicament now.

She'd have her husband's arm about her, facing her parents' death, yes. But not the soul-crushing loneliness that filled her.

She lay down on the settee, tucking her hands under the side of her face. She'd written to her best friend, now the Duchess of Wingate. Surely Aubrey would be able to help her. Or at least keep her company while she waited for her mourning period to end and her brother to return.

And after that? Would her brother help her find a match? He'd have his own new duties to fulfill, being the heir.

Perhaps Tinderwell was still available. She sat up. His Grace could write to the man on her behalf, ask for a meeting…

Distantly, she knew these were the acts of a woman who was desperately afraid, but suddenly, she needed some anchor to hold her in place. She was adrift, alone, and adventure sounded like the silly girl's notion who didn't understand just how delightfully secure she'd been.

"Miss Cranston," the butler spoke softly from the doorway. "I'm sorry to interrupt but you have visitors."

"Visitors?"

"Your father's solicitor." The butler cleared his throat. "And a second man who claims to be a friend of your brother's, Lord Robinson."

She stood, blinking several times, her gut giving a strange twist.

The solicitor she'd expected, though to be fair, she thought he'd not come calling until her brother had arrived.

But Lord Robinson…

She'd met him at Aubrey and Wingate's wedding six months prior, which felt like a lifetime ago. Her father had allowed her to attend without her mother, trusting Aubrey and the Duke to be her chaperones.

Robinson was tall, dark, and exceptionally handsome, his piercing green eyes the color of grass and mystery. Not that she'd spoken a word to him, despite him being her brother's childhood friend and a friend of the Duke. He was also a fair bit older than her—and a rake at that. Emily was well aware he'd never be interested in the likes of her.

Still, the trip had been a tantalizing taste of freedom that had elated Emily, though in this moment, her excitement seemed foolish. She ought to have stayed home. Found a suitor.

"Send them in," she said.

"Both of them?" the butler asked, his brow furrowing in an unusual display of feeling.

She lifted her hand still holding her kerchief. "Lord Robinson is a longtime friend of Ashton's. They attended Oxford together, both speaking fondly of the other." Emily had had very little to do with financial affairs, her parents sheltering her from such dealings. "I'm certain he'll be a great help during this meeting."

The butler gave a stiff nod of assent before he disappeared again, returning with both men. As today had been the funeral, Emily felt it proper to accept callers offering condolences.

But tomorrow, she'd begin her period of isolation as she mourned. She gave a shiver to think on it.

Lord Robinson entered, Mr. Barrow just behind him. Despite her thick crepe veil, Emily still noticed how large Lord Robinson was. He had to be more than six feet and his shoulders were so broad.

The urge to hide behind him welled up inside her though she forced her feet to remain in her spot next to the mantle.

"Miss Cranston," Lord Robinson said, giving a short bow as he took her hand in his. "Allow me to offer my sincere regret for your loss."

She gave a nod, her throat clogging with tears. "Thank you," she managed to whisper.

Mr. Barrow also bowed, offering similar words before his eyes strayed about the room. "No word from the new viscount?"

"No," Emily said with a shake of her head.

"Is there some relative that can join you here?" Lord Robinson asked, his brow furrowing in concern.

Mr. Barrow cleared his throat. "I've written to your great aunt and await a response."

Emily winced to think of the aging woman traveling. Her father's sister and widow to the Marquess of Delvin, she was too old to make such a journey. "Thank you for your concern but I'm not sure she'll come. I've written to the Duke and Duchess of Wingate. Perhaps when they arrive, they can escort me to her estate."

"Excellent," he said as Emily gestured for everyone to sit.

Lord Robinson sat next to her on the settee while Mr. Barrow took the seat across from them. A tea service was brought in, and she began to pour the cups automatically, as her mother had taught her to do.

"There are matters which we need to discuss," Mr. Barrow added between sips of tea. "But I'd prefer to have your brother here before we began."

"Then we shall be drinking a lot of tea, I think," she answered with a shake of her head.

Lord Robinson gave a small laugh, his gaze darting to her and then back to Mr. Barrow. "Is Miss Cranston provided for financially while she awaits her brother's return?"

"Yes," Mr. Barrow answered with a nod. "If he doesn't return—"

"Doesn't return!" Emily cried, the thought of her brother not coming back more than she could bear. Her vision grew grey around the edges, and she felt herself sway until a steadying hand came to her back, another grasping her fingers into a large palm.

She knew it was Lord Robinson's large hand that engulfed hers even as she had the urge to sink into the strength of his embrace.

"He'll return," came his quiet baritone. He sounded so confident, so self-assured, that she drew in a deep breath. She'd needed him to say that.

"Thank you," she answered, trying to draw in another deep breath, draw up the strength this conversation—this day—required.

Lord Robinson's hand was still on her back his large palm and long fingers nearly spreading from one side of her waist to the other. "Why don't you let me speak with Mister Barrow? I'll check in on you before I leave."

Oh, that sounded wonderful. She wanted to rise to the occasion, but she felt as though she were sinking. With a quick nod, Lord Robinson helped her up and out the door. "I'll just be in the study across the hall," she murmured as he stayed by her side, strong hand holding her still, helping her into the room and then into a chair.

"Close your eyes and rest. I'll be in soon."

She gave a quick nod and did exactly as he'd requested. She'd wished for freedom, but she could see now how wrong she'd been. What she needed was someone who could care for because she didn't have a clue how to care for herself.

———

JACOB CURSED himself a thousand times as he looked down at that damn veil covering her face. Emily was a fragile and protected beauty and on the few occasions they'd met, he could not deny that he felt her appeal. Intimately.

But until this morning, he'd kept his emotions well within check. He was not the sort of man who dallied with a viscount's daughter. Not an eligible one, anyway.

He liked his life just as it was, which was free of entanglement, devoid of commitment, and full of pleasure.

But after watching Emily this morning...

Not even he was cold-hearted enough to leave her to face this day alone. Was he going to regret this? Likely yes.

Jacob returned to the sitting room, Mr. Barrow looking decidedly irritable as he fidgeted with his glasses and adjusted his pocket watch. "My lord," the man began before Jacob had even sat. "There was little point in seeing the lady off."

"Why is that?"

"The details are not for you to discuss." The man somehow looked down his nose at Jacob despite being several inches shorter.

"Which details are those?" he asked, wishing for something stronger than tea. He knew it was a bad habit to drink as often as he did, but then again, life so often disappointed. He scraped a hand through his overlong hair.

"The ones that pertain to my client. I ought not to share them with anyone other than the new viscount." The man continued to fidget, pulling at his waistcoat and straightening his cravat. "The problem is that Miss Cranston has—" The man stopped, his lips pressing together.

Jacob sighed. He understood the solicitor's dilemma. Still, Jacob could not help Emily if he didn't know of any potential problems. And for some ludicrous reason, he was intent upon helping her.

At times, Ashton had felt like his only family, and he couldn't leave Ash's only living relative to flounder. He should pay Ashton back and this was his chance.

Besides, Emily seemed so fragile, and what was happening to her might lay even the strongest low. He'd not allow himself to get so tangled that he'd forget who and what he was, a man who did not allow himself to become attached to anyone.

Ever.

And he wouldn't to Emily. He was a seasoned rake, and she was just an innocent debutante. Hardly seasoned at all.

A small voice argued the point, he found her innocence refreshing, captivating even. Her grace and kindness were like a beacon and her beauty bewitching. But he turned that voice off. This was Ashton's sister and besides, innocence quickly faded and then he'd be left with the same sort of woman he knew well...

He wasn't meant to be tied to any female's apron strings.

Assured that he was not in danger of compromising his way of life, he gave Barrow an easy smile. "Mister Barrow, between you and I, I was in the process of negotiating with the viscount when his untimely death interrupted."

"Negotiating?"

Jacob gave a quick grimace that he quickly covered. He needed to know what was happening, which meant misleading Mr. Barrow into giving him information. Jacob would like to say that this was a first, but he was rather adept at fooling people into acting as he wished.

Which meant he knew the pitfalls to avoid.

"Emily and I..." He lifted his brows. He'd not say engaged. He was speaking to a solicitor, and he'd have preferred if the man inferred meaning rather than Jacob outwardly saying words he'd have to retract later. But he wanted Barrow to think it. He wanted the man to know that in Ashton's absence, Jacob was the man to trust.

Mr. Barrow's eyes widened, his hands smoothing down his middle. "I see."

Jacob could practically see the man calculating behind his spectacles, his pupils quickly moving left to right. And then he seemed to relax his shoulders. "All around, that makes everything easier."

Jacob had to agree.

Of course, he wasn't engaged to Emily, nor would he ever be, but Ashton would surely forgive the fib when he learned that Jacob only wished to protect the man's sister. Then again, perhaps this was the exact sort of behavior that made him so like his mother. But he pushed that thought aside. He was in it now, and he didn't see another way. "So tell me. What should I know?"

"Well, if you were negotiating a dowry then you're aware already. Aren't you?"

Jacob lifted his brows. Know what? But he didn't say a word. He found that silence often forced the other person to begin speaking.

Which was exactly what Mr. Barrow did. "But perhaps you'd not reached that point yet in your negotiations."

"Perhaps," he replied, again not committing to anything.

Mr. Barrow cleared his throat, eyeing Jacob. They were playing chess. Why? He waited for Barrow's next words as the man leaned forward. "The family hid it well, but Miss Cranston is very short on funds."

Jacob held completely still as though this information wasn't shocking in the least. Mr. Barrow watched him for several seconds before he eased back in his seat. So sweet, tempting Emily was without a protector or money? Fuck. "How short?"

Mr. Barrow shrugged. "She'll need to find a relative willing to provide for her until her brother can be found."

Inwardly he cursed a streak that might make a sailor proud. "But you just said she was fine."

"I didn't wish to worry her."

"What has been done to locate Ashton?" The man had gone on a tour of Europe a year before. He'd been expected to return to England months ago and the fact he wasn't here…

"I'm not privy to those details," Mr. Barrow's gaze shifted away, his mouth pinching.

Jacob's fist clenched against his thigh. The situation was worse than he'd imagined. "Rest assured, Mister Barrow, that while our engagement was not public, nor will it be until her mourning period is over, I shall see Emily well protected until her brother returns and can finalize our arrangements."

Mr. Barrow gave a quick jerk of his chin to acknowledge Jacob's words before he rose. "Excellent."

For the briefest moment, Jacob wondered at the distinct frown that marked Mr. Barrow's brow. Was there more he should know? Did Mr. Barrow have reason not to support Jacob's suit? It was fake, of course, but Mr. Barrow didn't know that. And the other man had likely heard of Jacob's reputation.

Hell, not even his own mother liked him, why would Mr. Barrow?

Then again, it was a risky maneuver claiming engagement and one that had the potential to backfire. Had this been too morally grey? He shifted, wondering if he'd really erred and put Emily at risk.

Jacob lifted his hand to show the man out and then started across the hall to see how the lady in question fared and decide what happened next.

Hell, even he didn't know. This was his first time pretending to be engaged.

CHAPTER TWO

Emily sat with her eyes closed, drawing in several deep breaths. Though she ought not, she flipped the veil up, allowing cool air to fan her face. She needed to think and breathe.

Mr. Barrow had said she had money, at least. That was a relief. But he'd also insinuated that her brother might not come back...

Her breath quickened, her pulse soaring with it as she pulled the comb that held the veil from her hair and tossed it to the side.

Next came the gloves. Those landed in a heap on the floor too and she stood, beginning to pace.

Her aunt would not be able to travel here, let alone help Emily attend a season once her mourning period was done. She'd hardly left her estate in the last decade, her joints bothered her so.

She pressed her hand to her stomach as she attempted to draw in a deep gulp of air.

"Emily." Robinson's smooth baritone washed over her, and she ceased pacing. His voice made her insides hectic, a not entirely welcome reaction and so she didn't look back at him.

"Is my brother dead?"

"Barrow doesn't know anything about your brother. Not any more than anyone else, anyway."

Her shoulders drooped, wilting in a bit of relief. "Do you think Ashton's dead?"

"No." Robinson said, moving closer. "He'll return home."

"What will I do if he doesn't?" she whispered. "My distant cousin will inherit the title. I've only met him once. Do you think he'll support me?"

There was a pause, Emily felt it in the air, his hesitation, and she turned around to finally meet his eye. "Lord Robinson?"

He let out a long breath, looking tired and a bit tense. What was wrong? "You might as well call me Jacob."

"Jacob?" she asked, studying his tense features. "Please tell me... what did you learn?"

Jacob shook his head even as he reached for her hand. The touch of his strong fingers sent a different sort of shock running through her. With his other hand, he swept back his overlong hair. "It's nothing—"

She let out a frustrated huff of air. Why did no one ever tell her anything? "I'm not a child."

"Emily, you are both young and sheltered," he answered with a frown. "It's better if you just do as I say."

That irritated her, which was a bit refreshing. She'd been sad, worried, fearful today. Anger made her spine snap straight. "You are not in a position to tell me to do anything."

His frown turned into a scowl. "I am protecting you."

"By treating me like a child?" she asked with a huff. In this moment, her old goal returned. She wished to know more, make decisions, take some control of her life. "I am nearly twenty and, it would seem, alone in the world. As much as I need protection, I could also use an education."

He still held her hand and his thumb made a sweeping motion across the back of hers. The gesture of comfort was in stark contrast to his scowl and a flutter of fear joined the awareness, tightening her body. Despite her strong words, she was worried what he might be keeping from her that would be worse than what she already knew.

"According to Mr. Barrow, you have very little funds."

She gasped, pulling her hand from his, her fingers coming up to cover her mouth. It couldn't be true. "No funds? How could that be possible?"

Jacob shook his head. "Possible? I've no idea. Were there any signs?"

"Like what?"

"Did your parents fight a great deal, seemingly about expenditures?"

She couldn't think of anything like that. "No. Not at all. They sent my brother on tour. They'd just purchased a new carriage. They were planning on opening the summer house and—" She stopped, searching her mind.

"Perhaps that was the issue? Overspending?"

Emily's eyes fluttered closed and a hollow, sick feeling settled in her stomach. Could this day get any worse? "I don't know. They didn't tell me any of it."

"We'll figure something out."

Her desire for independence deflated like a pig's bladder. Give her the safety of a match. "How am I going to marry now?" She had no family and no financial backing. Is that why her mother had wanted her to marry Tinderwell? Because they needed money?

Oh, how she truly yearned for the security she'd just lost. Guilt washed over her for forever wanting to be out from under her mother's rule. Had she wished this into being? It was a silly notion, but guilt still traveled through her for even thinking it.

"Well…" Jacob reached for her hand again, threading his fingers through hers. Her breath caught as her eyes widened. "About that…"

Was he going to propose? Her heart started racing again at the idea of being this man's wife. He was so big and handsome, older and so much more experienced in everything. She'd had this fantasy about him ever since they'd met. He'd hold her close, whisper in her ear, press her close. Of course, he'd never noticed her, not the way she did him. She was always Ashton's little sister, but the thought of curling into him filled her with an odd satisfaction. "What?" she asked, her voice catching on the single word.

"I told Mister Barrow that you and I were engaged."

She blinked up at him, trying to understand. "Are you proposing?"

"No." His lip curled as though the idea repulsed him. "I'm not the marrying kind. I lied for Ashton's sake, but…" He glanced at her like she was offensive in some way. Like the idea of wedding her pained him.

Her spine, already straight, stiffened. Obviously, he still didn't see her as anything other than his friend's sister and not even attractive at that. Hurt radiated through her. "Don't finish that sentence." And then she pulled her fingers from his.

"I just needed to get information from him."

Her lips parted. Did he not realize what he'd done? "But what if he mentions it to his other clients?"

"He won't. You're in mourning, so obviously we wouldn't be able to proceed until your brother returned and your mourning period ended. Besides, I only implied…"

"How does that help me?" she asked, her hands landing on her hips. "You can't escort me anywhere or it will confirm our engagement. You can't financially contribute. All you have done is create the possibility that I am ruined when people discover that you did not go through with our arrangement."

He scowled at her. "I am still a titled lord, handsome and sought after. My interest will help you."

She snorted then, falling deeper into the anger. It helped. "And so humble."

"I'm trying to help you."

She tossed up her hands. "Do you think my brother would honestly approve of this method of helping me?"

———

EMILY HAD A POINT. Actually, she'd had several.

And the woman he'd thought innocent to the point of being almost childlike was vanishing. In her place was a beauty with smarts and sass.

Fuck. He loved smarts and sass.

He'd felt a pull toward Emily since they had met. But all the characteristics he'd admired—her beauty, her grace and kindness—were amplified by her strength in this moment. She wasn't kind because she was weak. She was just deep down good...a bit of envy pulsed through him.

He wished he could be that clean.

Which only made him more certain he should keep his distance. He'd only ruin her with his own dark past. And she was not just a gentlewoman, she was the sister of one of his dearest friends.

Which meant the attraction he felt was completely unwanted. And deepening that want was a giant mistake. He could admire her beauty the way a man might enjoy a work of art and he could protect her for Ashton's sake.

But to like her...no, to really want her...that would make this whole situation so much more difficult.

"We can't leave you alone in this house with no method of providing for yourself."

She shook her head, her gaze growing thoughtful. "I've not heard a single stirring from any of the staff about accounts that haven't been settled. It's so odd."

But that news relieved him because it meant they had time. When creditors started calling, that's when the real problems started. He ought to know.

"We could quietly spirit you from the city. With your mourning period, you won't be missed."

She nodded. "I can go to see the Duke and Duchess of Wingate. They'd have me, I'm certain."

They surely would. The duchess was dear friends with Emily. And he'd known Wingate for years, so he trusted the man with this responsibility. And what was more, Wingate had the power, money, and standing to see Emily on the correct path no matter the circumstances.

"We could just travel with servants, but it would be better to have a real chaperone. As you mentioned...your reputation."

She grimaced. "I also mentioned that my only aunt is too old."

But another idea had struck him. "I've got an aunt who can do it."

"But she's not my aunt."

"Who's to know? Mister Barrow has surely never met your actual aunt."

Emily gaped at him. "Lie to the solicitor? Again?"

He shrugged. He found most rules...prohibitive. "He'll never know."

She shook her head, tsking. "You are dastardly, Jacob. Do you always lie this compulsively?"

There it was. Where he ended with most women. The part of him that had likely come from his mother just like his green eyes. "You're welcome for coming to your rescue."

She ignored that comment. "Did Ashton know this about you?"

"Of course he does."

"And he likes you despite your loose morals?" She cocked her head to the side as though she were understanding something about her brother or the world she hadn't known before.

"I have my charms."

"Devilish charms sure to land you and me in trouble if you're not careful."

"My mother would agree."

Her eyes rounded at that comment. And then they welled with tears.

He cursed himself. He ought not to have brought up mothers. Not today. Despite her goading and the fact she'd touched upon a topic he felt a certain sensitivity about, he didn't mean to poke at such a fresh wound.

Reaching for her, he pulled her into his arms, wrapping her in his embrace. He'd meant it as a gesture of comfort, but the moment she was pressed against him, he realized his mistake. She felt fantastic. Soft yet slender, exactly the right height, she fit against him perfectly. Her face burrowed into his shoulder and neck. He brought a hand up to her neck to hold her even closer as he rested his chin on top of her head. "It's going to be all right."

19

"I'm not sure it is," she sniffed into his cravat. "Maybe not ever again."

He remembered losing his father. The fear of becoming the baron, the loss of the one person who'd mentored him, at least.

Not that his father had been much help, but still.

"We'll find you a real husband, Emily. You're beautiful and accomplished and a lucky merchant will surely trade a dowry for your connections."

Her eyes lit at his words and for a moment, they captured him, the connection so strong he didn't even take a breath. Then she looked down, her long, dark lashes resting on the porcelain of her cheeks. "In the meantime, you're pretending to be my fiancé?"

"Just until I can transport you to Wingate and get some more information from the solicitor. I'll go to his offices again tomorrow and then I'll contact my aunt."

She gave a little jerk of her chin, all the fight gone. "All right." She lifted her head, her lashes fluttering before her chocolate brown eyes met his. She reached up, her fingers smoothing his cravat where she'd crumpled the garment. There was something so endearing in the gesture, her light touch both soothing and engaging. "Thank you for your help."

He used the pad of his thumb to wipe the last of the moisture trembling on her lashes. Her lips were softly parted, her eyes glassy but clear, her cheeks flushed.

The urge to kiss her stole through him. Why did he feel this protective need with her that he'd never felt with anyone else, all the while battling desire?

It mystified him.

Surely, he'd confused his loyalty to Ash with this woman? But he was old enough to know better than that. He needed to control these urges. They'd land him in even more trouble than he usually found himself.

Slowly, he released her, taking a step back as she curled in on herself, wrapping her arms about her own waist.

She appeared so forlorn that he had the urge to take her in his arms again. Hell, he nearly started to make her promises he knew he'd never keep.

CHAPTER THREE

JACOB TOOK the stairs two at a time, entering the establishment where he lived. Some lords kept a room at Madam Chamberlain's for the occasional night, but two years ago, it had become his full-time residence. He'd sold the townhome that had been in his family for generations to settle the most nagging of his father's debts. He'd been fortunate the property wasn't entailed.

He still had his entailed ancestral seat, Stoneleigh Manor, which barely managed to support itself. And the dowager house had been retained, along with a few others.

He was trying to make improvements to all his properties so they not only earned their own keep and decreased the debts but might someday make him enough profit to live as other lords did As Ashton and Wingate did. He was still a few years from that, however, so when in London, he lived here.

Jacob didn't regret his decision. He liked living among other people for the most part and he appreciated not being nagged by creditors. And living in a house of ill repute had a few advantages. Most notably willing women who were always available when a man had needs.

And today, he had a powerful one. Emily had started some ache inside him that had settled in his nether regions.

It was a solvable problem for a man of his station, and he started up the stairs, whistling as he went.

Give him a willing woman with experience and an understanding of the bargain they entered. Sex for money. No hopes of marriage, no judgment for not being a good enough man.

He opened the door and was greeted by Madam Chamberlain herself.

Once a great beauty, she still sparkled, there was just a whole lot more of her to love. Her brown hair sat piled on top of her head, her face lined with pleasant lines of age, her smile still infectious. She'd frequented Jacob's bed on many occasions, and he found himself considering doing so again.

The woman knew her trade well. And if he were honest, she'd been kinder to him than his own kin. But for some reason, the idea of being with her didn't quite satisfy. Was she too old? Too experienced?

"My lord." She dipped into a curtsey. "You're home early."

He gave a curt nod. Normally, he'd have gone to his club first, but he found the idea unsettling tonight. He needed some satisfaction and then some quiet time to think. "Long day."

She gave him a practiced smile of sympathy, her red lips parting, though the look didn't reach her eyes. "Anything we can to do help?"

The answer was *yes*.

But his gaze swung to the sitting room to the right where several women waited in various stages of undress and a frown pulled at his lips.

One was too thin, another not thin enough. Too old, too young, not pretty enough. Too blonde. Not one of the girls appealed. With a low rumble of frustration, he looked back at Madam Chamberlain. "A bath and dinner in my room will suffice."

Her brows notched, her eyes filled with a question she was too professional to ask, even as she nodded her understanding. "Of course, my lord. Anyone in particular you'd like to deliver them?"

The invitation was clear. And he'd meant to accept so why didn't he? "No, thank you. Though, I've an early appointment tomorrow morning so if you might see my jacket pressed before then?"

"Yes, my lord." She smiled demurely, all the while assessing him. "Anything else?"

"Yes." He ran a hand through his hair again, the long locks catching in his fingers. "My hair. Can someone trim it?"

"Esther can, she's quite good with her hands." Madame Chamberlain cocked her head meaningfully.

"Send her up before my bath and dinner then," he said as he started up the stairs. Making his way into his small room, he left the door open for the delivery of the tub even as he took off his coat and tugged off his cravat.

Removing the vest as well, he waited for the tub to be dragged in before he crossed to the desk and began penning a note to Mr. Barrow, then Wingate, and finally his Aunt Clara. The black sheep of the family, Clara had become an actress at the age of eighteen. She'd never married, though Jacob was certain she'd led an, er, colorful life.

Esther came in with a small leather roll in hand. "My lord?"

Esther was a short, pleasant-looking girl who giggled a great deal. She'd never been his sort, which actually suited his current mood. Pushing his chair into the middle of the room, he sat as Esther unrolled her tools, then began clipping his dark strands with fast, efficient scissors.

Giving him a hand mirror, he checked her work in the reflection before giving her a nod of approval. "Good. Thank you."

She rested a hand on his shoulder, leaning down so her own face peeked into the small mirror's reflection. Then her lips grazed the lobe of his ear. "Anything else I can for you, my lord? Anything at all?"

Her offer didn't tempt him in the least. And annoying as that was considering the ache in his balls, he gave her a quick *no* before sending her on her way.

He finished his letters and then sunk into a bath. Tomorrow he'd see what else Barrow knew. With any luck, he'd have Emily secured at Wingate's estate by this time next week and then, perhaps, he'd feel like himself again.

Because as he soaped himself up and scrubbed his skin, he rumbled with dissatisfaction. Emily was disrupting his wellbeing.

————

THAT EVENING, Emily wandered the halls searching for what, she knew not, but she found herself in her father's study.

Slowly, she ran her hand over the mantle. Normally, there would be a fire... She grimaced at the stark reminder that her father wasn't here. Her throat clogged with emotion even as her hand grazed his favorite leather chair. Swallowing down the lump, she moved behind the desk where her gaze landed on her father's strong box.

Her lips parted as she stared at it. Would she find any evidence of their financial troubles inside?

She needed a solid plan. Marriage seemed the best option. But to whom—a merchant, a lord? To decide, she'd have to learn more about her situation. Did she have money to pay an investigator to find her brother? Would Jacob help her with that?

She thought about the moment she thought he was proposing. Her heart had leapt with...she pushed away the thought before she could complete it. He had been clear that he didn't wish to marry, and she ought to find a man who wasn't quite so... She searched her mind for the proper phrase.... Perhaps morally fluid?

Opening the third drawer to the right, she easily found the key that sat in the back left corner. her hand shook as she reached for the small object. How often had she seen her father retrieve this same key?

Fingering the cool metal in her hand, she crossed to the box and inserted it into the lock. It clicked open and she lifted the heavy lid finding the contents neatly arranged inside.

Her father had always been tidy.

Thumbing through, she found various documents and memorabilia, some of which made her stomach twist with grief as she started at them. To the right, however, was an envelope labeled "Emily."

She gasped to see it and with a trembling hand, she reached down.

What would she find? A personal letter? An apology for the state of the barony?

Breaking the seal, she pulled the sheets out and at first stared with confusion. They were legal documents...

But then words popped out at her. Diamond. Quality. Value. She gasped, suddenly remembering.

Her mother's diamond ring. Originally her grandmother's, it was clear that it had been legally bequeathed to Emily. Was it worth much? Did it mean she wasn't destitute or was it just a nice memento from her mother's family?

Searching through the box, she found two more documents for two other jewels that belonged to her. A necklace and a pair of earrings that matched the ring. Taking the papers upstairs, she slipped into her mother's room and opened the drawers that held all her jewelry.

Running her hands along several pieces, she found the ones that had been labeled for her and pulled them from their velvet beds before carefully closing the drawers again.

Then, taking them to her own room, she set them on her vanity, staring at them. She remembered her mother wearing these, remembered the way they sparkled and winked in the candlelight.

A few tears slid down her cheek, but these were happier tears. She had these pieces of her mother that she got to keep.

Pulling out some of her stockings, she wrapped the jewels each in its own bit of fabric and then carefully tucked them in her drawer.

She didn't know why she didn't return them to her mother's room except when it was time for bed, she found herself holding the stocking with her mother's ring in the palm of her hand.

Drifting off to sleep, her parting thought was that when Jacob took her to see Aubrey, she'd bring the jewels. They were her birthright, her remembrance, and perhaps her salvation.

That thought helped her to relax as the world melted away.

———

THE NEXT NIGHT, Lucius Barrow sat behind his desk as candles burned around him. His most lucrative client was about to arrive.

And while Barrow worked with a fair number of the elite, he himself was a third son to a baron, he preferred clients of a more working class.

They had a certain scrappiness he admired. Tinderwell was the fourth son of a marquess who'd left his spare sons without a penny. He and Barrow understood each other.

Not like that detestable Lord Robinson. The man was a handsome waste. Barrow knew of his reputation. A rake and indebted drunkard, he did nothing but take from the people around him to suit his own needs.

So he didn't feel the least bit of guilt for lying to the man.

The front door opened and he stood, shuffling to the doorway of his private office to greet his guest in the waiting room. "My lord."

An older man looked at him, his steely eyes meeting Barrows. Still strong and imposing, his grey hair fell across his high forehead like an angry slash. "Let's dispense of the niceties and get started, shall we?"

See? That's what Lucius preferred. None of the flowery pompous conversation that was all for show. Give him a man who worked and knew the value of time. "Of course."

"Tell me everything about Lord Robinson and *my* Emily."

"He's making trouble, sir. Interfering with the plan."

"Start from the beginning."

Mr. Barrow stepped out of the doorway, inviting the other man in. "He's friends with the son. Says that he and Emily are engaged or soon to be."

His employer snorted. "He's never even been to the house before your meeting with him, so I don't see how that's possible."

Mr. Barrow lifted his brows though he didn't ask how the other man knew that Lord Robinson had never been to visit Miss Emily. "If the brother returns, my lie will be exposed."

"He won't return, not in time."

"You're certain?"

"By the time the new viscount comes home, you will have begun your life in the south of France, Mister Barrow. You're going to enjoy the sunshine far away from here."

Barrow gave an eager nod. Though he held no love for the peerage, he was glad that the new viscount wouldn't be harmed. Hurting a lord of the realm came with swift and serious consequences. "I'm sure I will."

"You've met with Lord Robinson twice now?"

"Yes, once yesterday when I visited Emily and again this morning. The funeral has surely brought him to Emily's side. So unfortunate, what happened to her parents." Mr. Barrow watched the man closely, looking for any sign that his employer might be involved. Much as Barrow liked working for him, he needed some assurance that his employer would keep his promises. And holding evidence of the other man's wrongdoing would surely provide Barrow with protection.

"And what does he intend to do with my Emily?"

"The aunt is coming to fetch her to bring her back to the county to mourn."

"Do me a favor and have them followed just to be certain." Tinderwell scratched his chin thoughtfully. "And have the house searched as well."

"Searched?" It was one thing to lie to a lord, another to break into one's home.

"Nothing will be taken, and no one will know we were there, but I want to confirm that the jewels are still on the premises."

Barrow cocked his head to the side. "Your goal in marrying the girl is to obtain her jewels?"

His employer shrugged. "I have been attempting to decide which is the main attraction and which is the added bonus. She is lovely."

Mr. Barrow nodded. It was not his concern really. Once his employer married Emily, he'd make enough money to leave England forever.

CHAPTER FOUR

THREE DAYS LATER, Emily smiled at the older woman before her, her brows notching up the slightest bit. Jacob's aunt, Clara Brownstein, was unlike any person she'd ever met before. Emily's mother had made certain that Emily never had a hair out of place, her dresses were always impeccable, her speech refined.

Mrs. Brownstein, named missus out of respect and not an actual marriage, wore an interesting combination of jade green and sapphire blue with dark pink accents. She had several flowers pinned in her haphazard hair and her lips had been painted a scarlet shade that only accentuated their wrinkles.

Her eyes, however, were as sharp as a woman a third her age and they assessed Emily as surely as Emily was looking at her.

Jacob stood next to his aunt, clearing his throat. "Aunt Clara, this is Miss Emily Cranston."

"A pleasure," Emily said hoping her smile appeared genuine enough.

"Pig's shit," the woman returned.

Emily blinked several times. "I beg your pardon."

Clara waved a bright red kerchief. "Don't bother pretending with me, girlie. My nephew told me the whole thing. Dead parents, missing

29

brother, no money, and an aging aunt who I am supposed to play." The other woman leaned forward. "Which I will be excellent at, by the way. Spent my entire life on stage."

Emily's lips parted as she considered a tactful way to disagree. Her father was a conservative man and his sister had been an English rose in her day. Clara could not be less like her actual aunt. "Will the role of baroness suit you?"

Aunt Clara frowned before her entire face changed a serious expression casting her features in a whole different light. "Does she speak most properly?" Aunt Clara asked, her accent growing finer. "And sit demurely and dress as blandly as possible?"

Emily had to smile. That was most definitely her aunt. "Bravo. That was impressive." But then her smile slipped again. Not because Clara wasn't exactly right or because she didn't appreciate the performance. But for the first time since her parents' deaths, she remembered what she didn't wish to become.

Clara had spirit and spunk. And Emily had been allowed none of that. At least not yet. She'd waffled since the funeral, did she wish for independence or security? Did she have a choice? It changed moment to moment.

Clara waved her hand. "Much as I appreciate adoring fans, I must confess that my participation is not contingent upon accolades." And she looked at Jacob giving him a meaningful stare.

Jacob sighed. "We don't need to discuss this now."

"Discuss what?" Emily asked.

"Tell her, already. Who knows? If it's as bad as you say, she might be joining me in the professional world, in which case, we should begin educating her on what makes the world turn immediately."

Jacob glowerd as he came to stand next to Emily, his hand sliding under her elbow. "Aunt Clara."

"You're very pretty." Aunt Clara assessed her up and down. "A beauty even. Nice chest too."

"Aunt Clara," Jacob repeated through gritted teeth.

"He's paying me to help, money he can ill afford because his father, my brother, was incompetent and his mother is a viper."

"Oh," Emily said, taking in all of that information as she turned to study Jacob. Was all of that true? He seemed so confident and self-assured all the time. "I'm sorry your mother is a viper. I understand. A bit. Mine was…"

"What?" Jacob asked, his gaze creasing in concern.

Emily let out a long breath. "Very confining."

"Of course she was, look at you." Clara waved a hand. "You should be falling apart and instead, here you stand here looking perfectly groomed and composed."

Emily frowned, looking down at herself. She was, wasn't she? It was just that getting ready gave her something to do. Some purpose.

"Have you had a chance to pack?" Jacob asked.

She nodded, waving toward the trunks that her maid stood next to. "Yes. All ready to go."

Beyond her maid stood the housekeeper and butler. Both people she trusted. Jacob's gaze flitted to the servants before they settled back on her. "Do they know anything?"

She'd asked but neither had any idea. "No. they didn't have any idea there was trouble in my parents' lives. What about Mister Barrow?"

Jacob's mouth pinched. "He had almost no information beyond what he first gave me."

Her own mouth turned down as she pressed a hand to her stomach. Tucked in her corset were the jewels from her mother. But there were several more in the case upstairs…

She didn't know who they belonged to legally. Were they part of the barony? Would they be seized when the assets were collected?

Would anyone miss them? Even know they were gone?

She remembered chastising Jacob for lying the other day, but today she didn't wish to follow the rules either.

And she had a perfectly viable solution as to how to pay Clara. If Jacob didn't have any money, then she'd have to help him. "You know. I've just remembered a few items that I forgot to pack. Can you give me a moment please?"

Jacob nodded as he brushed back his now-shorter locks of hair.

The cut made him even more handsome, and for a moment, she stopped and stared at his large masculine hand threaded through the dark locks. There was something so appealing about that hand and the arm to which it was attached.

And of course, the shoulders and the chest... Her gaze drifted down to his lean hips and then snapped back up as her body gave the strangest throb. "I'll be right back," she managed to stutter out a moment before she turned and fled.

———

"INTERESTING GIRL," Clara murmured from behind him as he watched the gentle swish of Emily's skirts.

"You don't mean that," he replied, knowing his aunt. The only people she ever found interesting were people who lived in the shadows.

"No. I likely don't." Clara came to stand next to him, tapping her chin. "Though there is something about her. A light in her eyes I recognize. She wants more or something different, despite following all the rules."

Jacob shook his head. "It doesn't matter. My job is to turn her over to the duke until her brother returns."

"And if he doesn't?" Clara asked, brows lifting. "It's odd he's not been heard from in months."

It was odd. He shifted his weight, worry making him restless. But there was nothing he could do until Emily was safe. "I'll get Emily tucked with the duke first —"

"You could marry her."

Jacob nearly choked. "And here I thought we understood each other."

"Your mother is convinced that you're going to kill yourself with your lifestyle and finally make your little brother the baron. Imagine how disappointed she'll be if you come home with a sweet bride who might birth an heir."

"Interesting point." He'd never considered that angle and the idea truly had merit.

"And the right bride might make your life easier."

"I've already told you, she's destitute."

"There is more to a marriage than money," Clara said. "And this is me talking. Besides..." Clara looked around the house. Jacob followed her gaze, seeing what she likely saw. Items of quality everywhere. Clocks. Vases. Highly polished wood and sparkling chandeliers. There was not one empty surface, no sign anything had been sold. "Hear me out. One, I don't know if there is reason not to trust the solicitor, but this does not appear like the house of a man about to go under."

Jacob frowned, his gaze sweeping over the entry again.

"It's understated, not lavish in its elegance. In addition, I made a few inquiries. The viscount is never seen at any of the clubs where I have friends. Not the gaming hells, not the houses of ill-repute, not even at gentleman's clubs. I suppose he could have made a bad investment but..."

"I see your point."

Clara gave him a meaningful stare, as though she weren't done making it, but someone else coughed slightly.

Jacob looked over to see the butler standing with his hands folded. "My lord."

"Yes?" Jacob asked. Was the man about to object to his plan to have his aunt and a maid as chaperones? Damn. That would make this more complicated.

But his questions were forgotten as the butler drew in a deep breath, glancing at the housekeeper who gave a quick nod. "I took the liberty of checking the household accounts we use to pay various services. They are flush with enough money to run this house for several months."

Jacob's brows drew together. "What the..."

"Interesting," Clara murmured.

It was far worse than interesting. Why would the solicitor have lied to him? But then again, no evidence as of yet supported the man's claim that the viscountcy was destitute.

For a moment he wondered if he ought to stay in London and investigate. He could check Emily's father's books. But was it his place?

Then again, he was taking Emily out of the city with this clandestine method so perhaps it was warranted.

Emily came down the stairs once again, clutching her reticule to her chest.

She looked a bit wild, her eyes wide and he stopped to stare at her. The effect was not unattractive.

Clearing his throat, he looked over at the butler again. "Emily could use a refreshment before we begin our journey. Perhaps Aunt Clara could rest in the sitting room just there and you could show me to your father's study. We'll take tea there."

Emily's eyes widened even further but she softly answered. "All right."

He looked over at the butler who jerked his chin in acceptance, the look almost imperceptible.

CHAPTER FIVE

EMILY SAT in the chair of her father's desk as Jacob looked over her shoulder.

She'd thought that they'd come in here so that Jacob could raid the brandy. But what was actually happening was a complete surprise.

They were studying her father's books.

Which ought to have concerned her. Jacob did not have the best reputation and she was a woman alone.

But of all the things she was scared of currently, Jacob was not one of them. "It doesn't make sense," he murmured his breath tickling her ear.

"What doesn't?"

"These books show steady profits and expenditures that are well within the viscountcy's means. So did the last. But why would Mister Barrow lie?"

Emily shrugged. "To frighten you away?"

Jacob stiffened behind her before her let out a menacing growl, the rumble moving through her. "Christ. You're right."

Was she? No one ever told her that she'd made some great insight. It was...refreshing. "Really? You think? Do you think he knows of your reputation and that's why?"

"Maybe." Jacob withdrew, a look of pain tightening his features.

Did he not like the way people saw him? She could understand that.

She rose, closing the book. "Have we found what we needed?"

Jacob gave a tight nod. "Once I've got you in Wingate's care, I'll come back to the city and investigate this matter further. I trust him and so did your parents. You'll be safe."

"Thank you," she murmured softly. She knew he did all of this for Ashton, but she still appreciated his care. He'd done more for her than anyone else since her loss and this journey had certainly distracted her when she'd needed it most.

"You're welcome," he answered, cocking his head to the side. "And just out of curiosity, what do you know of my reputation?"

She lifted one shoulder, casting her gaze to the ground. "Well. I've heard the word rake bandied about a time or two."

He stepped up to her, his forefinger coming up to her chin to lift her face until she was looking in his eyes again. "Emily."

His green gaze seemed to penetrate her soul, her breath held captive in her lungs as she waited. "Yes?"

"You're safe with me, I can assure you. I would never hurt you. Ashton—"

"Yes, yes." She ignored the bit of hurt that pulsed through her chest. "You'd never do anything to hurt him. I know." Why did that bother her?

"Right." His mouth pressed into a thin line. "Now let's leave, shall we? Our departure has already been delayed."

She turned for a moment, walking in front of him, before spinning back. Only he'd already taken a step forward and she found herself crashing into his chest, his arms wrapping about her to steady her.

"Oh, Jacob, I'm sorry." Her chin tilted up and then she was captured in his gaze again, only this time he was so close that his scent wrapped about her. It was masculine with tones of sandalwood but there was a hint of cinnamon that had her breathing deeply.

And then there was the sight of his lips, so close and so tempting.

"There is nothing to apologize for. Did you forget something?"

She nodded, taking a careful step back but she instantly missed his heat. Giving herself a little shake, she reached into her reticule and pulled out a ruby bracelet. "I got this for Aunt Clara."

He blinked several times, looking down at the twinkling jewel. "Clara?"

She nodded. "As payment. I've no idea what's it worth but—"

"I don't need your assistance in paying my aunt." His voice had taken on a hard edge that had her taking another half step back, her brow scrunching in confusion.

"But," she said, then licked her lips. "She's coming for my benefit."

He reached for the bracelet and then her reticule, tossing the bracelet inside again. "First, you've no idea what that piece is worth. Second, you might need it for yourself, we'll still not entirely certain. Third, what if someone misses it and wants an accounting of where it went?"

"I'll tell them I buried my mother in it."

"Oh, that's not bad, actually." But then he gave his head a hard shake. "And last, but most important, I take care of you. You do not need to care for me."

Her mouth opened and closed. Why would that be? It made no sense. "But you don't have any funds. Clara said—"

"I know what Clara said," he barked back, making her spine snap straight.

"You don't have to be rude. I was trying to help."

"I don't need that kind of help, not from you." And then he stepped up to her, his hand at her back, turning her back toward the door and propelling her forward. "I will see you to Wingate, I will pay my aunt, and then I will come back here to discover why Barrow is giving us the run around."

"And what is my job?" she asked, stopping in the hall until she forced him to stop as well.

He scowled. "I don't know. Your job is to—"

She waved him off. "Let me guess. To look pretty. To behave myself. To do as I'm told." Her booted foot gave a small stomp under her skirts. "Look where that got me," she said, opening her arms to show her travelling clothes.

Then she started back down the hall again toward the entry, leaving him standing in the same spot. In this moment, she felt herself leaning toward a decision for her future. She was not going to be a bystander in her own life.

But she stopped and spinning about, started back for her father's study.

"Where are you going?" he asked turning to follow.

"I'm bringing books and correspondence to review."

"Review for what?" He followed behind her as she pulled the key for the lock box from the drawer and opened the lid.

"I don't know yet, but I'll start learning about the affairs that concern me during the drive and I'll continue to do so when we reach the duke and duchess's home. I'll not be caught unaware again."

Aunt Clara appeared in the door next to Jacob then. "Now, see," the other woman said with a small smile. "Her eyes told the real story."

Emily didn't know what that meant but she didn't think on it or ask as she began searching the box.

Pulling out groups of letters and books, she waved hand. "See if you can find a crate."

"A crate?"

She looked up then. "For the papers. For our investigation. I'm assuming this will give you a place to start when you return to London."

His lips parted as he stared at her for a moment. "A crate." And then he turned to do as she bid. A wave of pride washed over her. Finally. Someone had listened to her.

She returned to the box, wondering if she'd upset him. He'd been so angry—and he was the last person she wished to make angry—but all the same, she needed to be part of this.

"Well done, girlie," Clara said leaning against the door.

"Why do you say that?" she asked, pulling out a stack of letters that all seemed to be from Barrow.

"You've got his hackles up and he's starting to froth. Keep pushing. Unsettle him."

Emily lifted her head. "Why would I want to do that?"

"Men like a challenge. Give him one."

She didn't want to challenge Jacob. She wanted his help.

But then the idea of them both being heated, the image of dark looks and heavy breathing, made her whole body tense up. She straightened. "Hackles and froth?"

Clara gave a low, husky laugh. "I'll teach you a few things. It will make the journey less dull."

Emily cocked her head. She was very interested in learning whatever Clara might be able to teach. No matter which future she decided upon, she was certain that Clara's education would prove useful.

―――――

JACOB ATTEMPTED to sit still as the carriage ambled down the road. It would take the rest of today, all of tomorrow, and a good portion of the next day to reach Wingate's estate in Northampton.

Which meant he was trapped in a very small space with the lovely and enticing Emily.

He'd let her get under his skin earlier, he knew that. Odd because he never cracked. Not when his mother claimed he was good for nothing or that his brother Eric should be the baron and not Jacob.

He'd learned to tune her out years ago. And he'd applied that skill to nearly every facet of his life. For example, he didn't get angry when he had to sell a property and men chuckled behind their cheroots at the club.

He didn't fuss when fans snapped and whispers followed him. Nor was he concerned when men didn't include him in their business's ventures because they thought him incapable. Never mind that the debt had been his father's, not his.

But something in Emily thinking that she needed to provide for him had riled him. He was a man. A man who was perfectly capable of providing and protecting a woman who needed it. The fact that she didn't think so...

Well, it had made anger bubble up inside him. He'd been tempted to insist that he was slowly improving his financial position. He normally didn't care what others thought but with her he'd grown...defensive.

Not only did she make him question himself with her assumption about his character, but she'd attracted him with her beauty and resolve. Even now, her scent filled his carriage, an intoxicating mix of floral notes with just a touch of sweet that made him sure she'd taste delicious.

Her pale skin glowed in the dim light, her lips softly parted as she glanced out the window, her fingers softly holding the curtain.

She'd pinned her lush brown hair away from her face. A thick shiny mass he could picture tumbling down her back.

"Tell me," Clara started, giving him an eye. "How did you know Emily's brother?"

"We attended school together." He looked at his aunt. He didn't add that Ash had taught him about what it meant to be loyal and true. They weren't traits that featured heavily in his family.

"Oh yes. I remember him. Same warm brown hair and eyes as his sister." Clara looked over at Emily whose mouth had pinched into a pained, straight line.

"He was a very good friend to me." Jacob remembered a time that he'd snuck out of the school after hours. He'd gone to meet a girl. A rake even then, but it was Ashton who'd gotten him back in and covered his absence so that he wasn't expelled.

Emily gave a very tight nod. "And brother to me."

He could hear the pain in her voice. Briefly he wondered if he'd hold up as well as she had considering the circumstances. Emily was a fighter, he realized, all in her own ways. "We'll find him as soon as we have you settled."

Her breath caught as she leaned forward. "Do you mean it?"

"Of course." He sat up a little straighter, wishing he could touch her. Lace her fingers through his. Run his thumb over the silky skin on the back of her hand.

But he could do none of those things and so he watched the scenery amble by for hours until they finally reached an inn where they could stop for the night.

After escorting the ladies inside, he booked each of them a room and then they settled in a private dining room where they had a very quiet dinner. Emily had hardly said a word since they'd left London and Clara seemed deep in thought. He was too. Had he deserved Ashton's friendship back then? Did he now? He was trying to do right by Emily, but thus far he'd lied and cheated her away from the city. Then again, Barrow didn't deserve the truth.

Finally, Clara rose, excusing herself to retire upstairs. She gave him a meaningful stare before she left the private dining room.

Much of Emily's food was still on her plate and he leaned forward, softly urging. "Sweetheart, you should eat."

Emily blinked, her gaze focusing on his. "Oh. Sorry. I've been distracted."

"Do you want to tell me what's bothering you?"

She shook her head. "I thought I hated ambling about my family home alone. And I did. But leaving is somehow worse. Like I'm losing pieces of them." She pressed a hand to her stomach.

He winced. "I lost my father too. Several years ago. We weren't close but I still felt adrift."

Her eyes clouded with pain. "Did the feeling go away?"

"It did." He did reach for her hand then, threading her fingers through his. "I'm sorry I gave you a hard time this morning. I..." Did he explain?

Her gaze lifted to his. "Don't be. We're similar..." She swallowed then. "You're a bit like my family now and that means we're bound to fight."

He gave a terse nod, but those words didn't sit quite right either. They should. He was doing this out of loyalty to her brother. He'd been like a brother to Jacob, which meant Emily should be like his little sister. But she wasn't and Clara's words about marrying Emily came back to him.

Which was ridiculous. He lived in a brothel. He drank and whored and he'd promised himself that he'd never subject himself to marriage. Not after what he'd seen happen between his parents. He let the world think him a reprobate because it kept anyone from holding him to standards.

He slid his fingers from Emily's. "Family does fight."

She nodded and then dutifully lifted her spoon. "Tonight, I'll start looking through the documents that I brought from my father's office."

He wanted to object. She needed rest. But he needed some distance. "I'll wait until you're done eating and then I'll escort you upstairs."

She took a few more bites, then pushed her chair back. "I'm ready."

He stood too, reaching for her hand once again. He shouldn't picture what it might be like to bring her not to her own bed but his.

But he did anyway. Christ. It was going to be another long night.

CHAPTER SIX

EMILY SAT READING letters until her eyes crossed, not that she'd made any progress in their investigation into her affairs. They were filled with the driest information on ledgers and number of sheep. Still a picture was emerging. Her father's holdings were healthy in terms of production and finance. Mr. Barrow was a liar.

She blew out in a long, frustrated stream of air. She'd be so relieved to reach Aubrey and Wingate. They'd surely know what to do.

A knock sounded at the door and she rose, crossing the room. "May I help you?"

"It's me," Aunt Clara called. "May I come in?"

Emily opened the door, stepping back to let the other woman in. Clara had changed, her outfit more sedate, her hair neater. She sashayed into Emily's room, her gaze flicking over the papers. "Learn anything of interest?"

"That I ought to have paid more attention sooner," Emily said, then grimaced as she looked down at the sheets.

Clara crossed to the bed, lounging back on it. "It is really amazing what happens when you take control of your own life."

"Is that what you did?" Emily asked, as she replaced the letter she'd been reading into its envelope.

"Yes. My brother, Jacob's father, was terrible with money and he'd married a woman intent on spending as much as she could. I could have married, of course. Found another man to take care of me but I was too restless for that. I wanted freedom, a lack of confinement, and control."

Emily stopped straightening the papers as she glanced over at Clara, fascinated by the woman's words. She'd had moments where she felt the same. "Do you like living on your own?"

"Not always," Clara answered, looking up at the ceiling. "But I would have liked being married less."

Emily nodded. She hadn't wanted to marry either. That wasn't true. She'd like to marry, just not the men her mother had paraded in front of her. But she wanted to be with a person who respected her. Who allowed her to think and participate in her own life not just wish for her to be a pretty ornament. "It's not marriage I object to. It's not having a say in who the man might be that bothers me. Or the choices he makes that affect me. I'm tired of being treated like I'm useless or unintelligent."

Could she have both? Some measure of control and the security of a good marriage? It was a tempting thought…

"It's difficult to find a man who'll consider your mind equal to his. Even when it is."

Emily stared at the window, knowing that Clara was right. "My last suitor, Lord Tinderwell, was a merchant by trade. He was different from other men who'd courted me. He listened more, I think. Granted, he looked at me as though he didn't quite understand me, but at least he listened." His gaze had always disconcerted Emily, though she didn't understand what caused the feeling. "But he…" She shook her head, remembering the events that had transpired six months prior.

"What?" Clara asked, bringing her back to the present.

"He had eyes that disconcerted me, and one night he tried to kiss me. It frightened me and I refused to see him after that."

"Are you questioning your reasons now?" Clara asked.

Emily frowned. He'd been older, not handsome but arresting, and there had been an air of danger about him. "When my parents first died, I was afraid to be alone. I wished I'd married him."

But even after only a few days, she recognized that much of those feelings were desperation. Tinderwell had never made her feel like... Her breath hitched to think of Jacob. She'd not experienced any emotion like that before and so she'd had no comparison to weigh her feelings for Mr. Tinderwell at the time. "But that wasn't real affection. I was afraid and I wanted comfort."

Clara sat up. "Emily. Don't be afraid to ask for the moon and expect a man to give it to you. You'd be surprised how powerful it can be to know your worth."

Emily stared at the other woman, wondering about those words.

Aubrey had been a seamstress who'd married a duke because she'd been brave enough to demand he respect her.

She nipped at her lip, wondering how a woman demanded without pushing a man away. She opened her mouth to ask when a tapping noise at the window caught her notice. Strange. They were on the second floor.

Clara, hearing it too rose from the bed, crossing to the window and peering out into the night.

"Do you see anything?"

Clara shook her head, turning away when the noise sounded again.

Emily jumped, Clara cringing away. "Blow out the candle."

Emily did as Clara asked.

"I'm going to get Jacob."

"Good idea." Emily rose too, tucking herself next to the wall as Clara left. Was she being silly? It might have just been a branch or a bird or...

The window gave a definite rattle as though someone were trying to open it. She gasped and then covered her mouth with her hand, shrinking closer to the wall. Her other hand pressed to her corset where the jewels were tucked inside.

Her door burst open, Jacob filling the doorway for a moment before he let out a rumble, his gaze not on her but on the window.

And then he strode across the room in an instant, throwing open the sash and leaning out into the night even as he pulled a pistol from his waistband.

She held back a scream as she saw the weapon. Squeezing her eyes shut, she heard him snarl as the hammer clicked back and then an eerie silence filled the room. Emily's throat clogged as Jacob continued to scan the darkness. After what felt like minutes, but was likely only seconds, she unclogged her throat long enough to croak out. "Jacob?"

"Shhh," he murmured. "It's all right. I'm here." He still scanned the darkness, his jaw hard, his body large and broad even as he comforted her.

Her breath hitched as she inched closer to him. "Who was that?"

"I don't know," he answered, straightening away from the window and closing it tightly once again. He still looked out into the darkness. "But pack up your things."

"And take them where?" she asked, stopping a foot from him so that she remained out of view. Did he mean to leave the inn? Find another?

"To my room."

"Y-y-your room?" she asked shivering with a new apprehension. It was one thing to speak privately with Jacob, but to be in a room alone with him…sleeping?

He finally looked away from the opening and toward her. Without the candle there was hardly enough light to see his features, but she could feel his gaze, and her skin prickled with awareness. "I can't keep you safe if you're in another room."

Safe. The word unwound something inside her or perhaps that was his tone. Deep, masculine, full of some assurance that he was here to protect her. He was right, of course. The man who'd come to her window was a danger.

But as she looked at the breadth of Jacob's shoulders, the way his strong jaw flexed she felt her stomach flutter with some unnamed need. Who was going to protect her from the feelings swirling inside her?

———

HAVING Emily in his room was certain to be a small form of torture.

Her small fingers curled into his as he led her down the hall, her breath hitching as he opened the door.

She'd decided to leave her trunk in her room, but the crate of papers was tucked under one of his arms, her reticule dangling from her wrist.

"Jacob?" Her voice trembled as she stepped into the room, her fingers flexing in his. "Do you think he'll try…"

Quietly, he closed the door and set down the crate. Then, because he couldn't resist, he pulled her close, something he'd meant not to do. He didn't want to make the situation any more grey by adding more intimacy. It was bad enough he was in his room alone with her.

And Ashton was still in the forefront of his thoughts, but his allegiance was slowly shifting to include Emily. Perhaps even more powerfully. He felt this intense need to protect what was so beautiful about her.

If anyone other than Clara knew, he'd have to marry her for certain.

She brought a trembling hand to her forehead, his gut twisting for different reasons. She was so vulnerable. Both in situation, but also as a fragile beauty, she'd been left alone. Drawing in a deep gulp of air, he resolved to do whatever was necessary to keep her safe.

That included putting his attraction to the side in order to make certain no one harmed her. "Try to hurt you? I would never let anyone do that. Ever."

"Really?" she breathed even as he eased away.

He didn't want to. He'd like to keep holding, settle her closer still.

But with her feminine aroma permeating his senses he pulled further away as he cleared his throat. "Promise."

He crossed the room and blew out his candle, casting the room into near darkness. He heard Emily set her reticule on the table and then sit on the bed. He looked over at her, noting that even in the dim light she appeared awkward and uncomfortable, her movements jerky as she tried to settle.

It almost made him smile. So innocent.

"I think it best you sleep in your clothes…at least for tonight."

She gave an absent flutter of her hand. "Agreed."

"We'll leave very early tomorrow to try and make good time."

She didn't look at him, plucking at the coverlet on the bed. "Why do you think that man was at my window?"

"Most likely he was a petty thief," Jacob said as he stationed himself next to his window, peering out into the night. Was the man still prowling about or had Jaco frightened him off?

Emily let out a small sigh, seeming lost in thought, even as Jacob straightened away from the window. "Have you still got that bracelet in your reticule?"

"What?" Emily looked up at him, blinking. "Oh. Yes."

He frowned. Emily looked every inch the lady. Would someone have targeted her? Could they have known she'd have jewelry or was it all just a coincidence?

He grimaced. He should have told her to leave the bracelet at home. Why didn't he? He was supposed to be the one protecting her. He never did seem to get these sorts of things right. A man who understood how to care for others likely would have thought of that.

He remembered his mother tossing similar accusations at his father. She'd been convinced her husband couldn't do a thing right. What made it worse was her accusations might have been on target. What did that say about his mother's opinion of him?

Emily unlaced her boots. He almost leaned down to help her, but he kept his eyes forward out the window as he listened to the sound of her slipping them off.

She lay down on the bed, remaining on top of the covers as she tucked her feet under her skirts. "I will say, all this adventure can distract a person from grieving."

A half smile curled his lips. "I bet it can. Grief always comes out eventually."

"That's true," she said, tucking her hands under her head. "At least I think it's true. I've never lost like this before."

"I can't imagine..." he murmured, clearing his throat. "Losing my father was difficult but even worse was the mountain of problems he made mine after he passed away."

"The debt?" she asked softly and he gave a tight nod.

"I've been working my way out of it. But as much debt as I've removed, it's still a noose around my neck."

"Why not marry?" Emily asked, propping her hand up on her elbow.

For the briefest second, he thought she meant herself. His heart began to pound in his chest as he looked over at the curve of her hip, the alluring line of her body, as she rested her head on one of her hands. "Marry?"

"Yes. Some girl with a large dowry who will wipe your debts clean."

Did it irritate him that she hadn't been speaking about herself? How odd was that?

"I already told you. I'm not the marrying kind. Not after watching my parents. My mother bore my father two sons, though how that's even possible has always been a mystery to me. They hated each other passionately. She didn't like me much better. But to me marriage has always seemed like a prison."

Emily sat up again, the soft rustle of her skirts whispering through him. "That is terrible. My mother was ceaselessly in everyone's business. It was maddening at times, but she did love us and my father. I'm trying to imagine what it would be like if she didn't."

He turned to her then, her soft words soothing some inner wound. Emily hadn't rejected his notion, or suggested he might somehow be to blame. A feeling of warmth swelled in his chest as their eyes met. "Thank you for not insinuating it's my fault."

Emily softly shook her head. "I sometimes thought my mother was in my business all the time because I..." She swallowed then. "Because

I'm not capable. But I hope it was about her and not about me. Or at least, not all about me."

His lips parted as he stared at her. Did she really understand the self-doubt he battled too? That deep-down voice that said his mother didn't like him because he didn't deserve to be liked. That there was something wrong with him. "I promised myself never to marry," he confessed. "What if I married someone like my mother or what if…" And then he shuddered, despite himself, one of his deepest fears rising to his lips. "What if she's right and I am no good?"

Emily was off the bed in a moment and in his arms. He wrapped her up in his embrace, more glad than he could express to be holding her. He dropped his cheek to the top of her head, squeezing his eyes shut. "From where I stand," she whispered. "You are one of the best men I know. Without you…" she tapered off. "Don't believe her, Jacob. Don't let her do that to you."

And then she slipped from his arms again and returned to the bed.

A thousand words of gratitude, affection, even desire rose to his lips, but he bit them all back.

He watched her as she lay down, watched as she fell asleep. Her face relaxed, looking just as beautiful but even more innocent.

Could she possibly know what sort of man he was? Did her words have merit? Deep inside, he wanted to believe them, but he wasn't certain he could. He hadn't believed Ash when his best friend had uttered the same words at his father's funeral. What was it with the Cranstons believing in him? Why had he let Ash drift away from him in the last ten years? And what of Emily? He'd have to let her go too…

At some point, he lay down on the floor next to the bed. He almost hated to do it, he couldn't see her from this vantage point, but he needed at least a few hours of sleep before the journey tomorrow.

Her hand dipped over the side of the bed, and without hesitation, he lifted his own up and slipped his fingers into hers. Her skin was silken and so soft against his that he threaded their fingers together and promptly fell asleep.

CHAPTER SEVEN

EMILY WOKE, her arm numb. Her eyes cracked open and her head lifted the smallest bit to see what the problem was, but as she lifted her head, she realized that her lower arm was hanging off the bed and attached to something very heavy.

Lifting up further, she peaked over the edge and nearly gasped at the sight of her fingers joined with Jacob's.

Oh, this man. She studied his features in sleep, noting that even softened, the hard masculine edges of his features were beyond arresting.

Her breath caught. Was any man ever more handsome or more wonderful than this one?

"Good morning," he rumbled, not opening his eyes. "Get any sleep?"

"I did," she whispered back, fully awake in a matter of seconds. How had she ever slept with him so close and with their hands joined? She wished she'd been awake to appreciate this small gift.

"Me too," he squeezed her fingers and then gently removed his hand from her grasp, pushing himself off the floor and into a sitting position. "Though my back is not thanking me now."

She swung her legs over the edge and scurried behind him. "I'm so sorry," she gasped even as she reached for his shoulders, beginning to rub them.

He looked over his shoulder, his eyes meeting hers in the dim light of dawn. Her hands stilled. "Do you not like it?"

"No. It's wonderful," he said even as he pushed up again. "I'm going to collect some bread and cheese so that we might eat in the carriage. I want to leave as soon as possible."

She gave a quick nod. "All right." She looked down, not wanting him to see the disappointment surely coloring her eyes. To do something, she began shaking out her skirts.

He touched her wrist, stopping her. Lifting her chin, their gazes met again, as he reached up to brush his fingertips over her cheek. "Would you mind if we drove through the night?"

She shook her head. "No. Not at all. I'm eager to reach my friends."

He grimaced then, looking pained. "I'll keep you out of harm's way until then."

"I have every confidence," she whispered, her hand covering his. "But sleeping in a place where thieves don't require you to guard me would be nice."

That made his face relax, his lips tugging up into a smile. "Guarding you was not the worst task ever."

Her breath caught as her lips parted, their eyes locking. She wanted to move closer. To press against him. With a deep intake of breath, she realized she wanted to kiss him. What would it be like?

A knock sounded at the door, interrupting the moment, both of them stepping back from the other.

"Jacob?" Clara called.

"Coming," he answered as he turned away and moved to the door. Opening it, he let Clara in. "We're leaving as soon as I can have the horses hitched."

"Good," Clara answered. "Go get it done while I stay here with Emily."

He gave a quick nod and then disappeared.

Clara turned to her. "Now tell me. What happened last night?"

Emily's brow furrowed. "You mean the man coming to the window?"

"No, I mean you sleeping with my nephew."

Emily gasped, her stomach dropping to her toes. "He was on the floor the entire night."

Clara frowned. "Really?"

"Really," she answered, holding out her hands.

Clara cocked her head. "You're certain I don't need to tell the duke to insist that Jacob marry you."

Now Emily was confused. "You're not insinuating that I was attempting to trap him?"

"No. I was insinuating that you should."

Emily blinked several times. "I beg your pardon?"

"That clawing mother of his has him convinced he's not husband material. Her manipulations are always multilayered. But an heir would be the quickest way to cut her out of the conversation completely. She's hung her hat on her other son becoming the baron and putting her back into a position of power in the barony. I would like nothing more than to see you and he wed."

"He doesn't want—"

"Don't be a fool, girl. I've seen a thousand men want a thousand women and that one wants you."

She shook her head. "He's Ash's friend. He's just trying to be loyal…"

Clara gave her a pat on the cheek. "My dear. Think long and hard about what you want from Jacob because, if we're being honest, it's within your power to receive all of it."

Emily seriously doubted that was true. The older, rakish, titled lord was not going to give little, meek Emily Cranston whatever she wished. The idea was absurd.

Wasn't it?

———

THE SCENERY MIGHT HAVE BEEN lovely, but none of it compared to the woman sitting across from Jacob. Emily's profile was lit by the sun as she stared out the window.

He tried to decide if she'd been more beautiful by moonlight or sunlight and finally determined that he'd need to see her in both several more times to decide.

Clara began to hum, though when he looked at her, he realized that she was staring back at him.

He shifted, grimacing, knowing he'd been caught studying Emily. Clara quirked a brow, looking both attractive and oddly not like herself in her lack of makeup and her hair coifed in simple style. She looked like a matron, the sort that might tell him what he ought to be doing with his life.

And right now, he knew what she'd say. *Marry Emily.* He did look out the window then, pretending to watch the bucolic fields roll by, intimately aware of every shift that Emily made until he thought he might go mad.

He was a seasoned rake, for Christ's sake. How had Emily, an innocent, gotten so completely under his skin?

But it was that innocence he found so refreshing. She was honest, kind, and sweet. It made him want to fight the world to protect those qualities. And here she wished to be more mature.

He supposed everyone did, but he'd like to see her maintain her wonderful qualities a little longer. Some of them, he had this ridiculous wish to keep them safe forever.

And then there was his attraction to her. It pulsed through him like nothing he'd felt before, at least not that he could remember. It didn't help that she was always looking at him like he mattered.

Like, to her, he might just be worth a damn.

His fingers clenched in the curtains as a muscle in his jaw ticked. Why had he not realized that he'd wanted some woman to look at him the way Emily had this morning? And the words she'd spoken last night about his mother being wrong...

It was as though she were pushing at his soft spots, finding the ways into his... He didn't finish that thought as he looked over at his knuckles and realized they'd turned white around the gauzy fabric.

He forced his fingers to relax.

"What shall we talk about?" Clara asked, sounding very amused. "The fine weather? The good company?"

Emily looked away from the window, smiling at Clara. "Rain would make this entire affair much more difficult."

Rain? Weather? He snorted. That's what they were going to discuss? "Ladies."

But the sound of distant hooves caught his notice.

There seemed to be more than one horse and they were moving quickly. His gaze narrowed as he thumped the wall behind him. "Pull off into that patch of woods ahead. Hurry."

The carriage sped up, the black vehicle, pulling off the road and into the patch of woods.

He was out of the carriage in a moment, leaving a stunned Emily and Clara in the vehicle as he ducked through the trees back to the road.

Three men came barreling down the road on horseback, speeding by. His gaze narrowed as he began darting through the woods, to follow, as they drew up their mounts at the edge of the woods.

"Where did it go?" one called to the others, slapping his hat on his leg.

"Heard it speed up, think they heard us?" Another scanned the road.

Jacob reached for his pistol, pulling it from his waistband. These men were talking about his carriage, he was certain of it. What was more, they were attempting to follow him. Had they also tried to break into Emily's room?

But why?

"We'd better try to catch up," the third finally spoke. "We can't lose them."

Jacob waited until they kicked their horses into motion and then he strode back to his carriage. "Turn it around," he barked before climbing inside.

"Turn what around? The carriage?" Clara asked. "Why?"

He didn't want to frighten Emily, he really didn't but she also deserved to know what was happening.

He raked a hand through his hair. "Those men are attempting to find us."

Both women gasped even as the carriage began to move, following the small track through the woods so that it could reverse direction on the road.

"What will we do?" Clara asked, her voice catching as a hand came to her throat.

Emily's face had gone pale and he found himself reaching for her hand. "I don't have a choice. We'll have to…" He gave a shudder. "Stop at my mother's."

Clara choked. "Why? Are we that close?"

"Very close," he gritted his teeth. "And I can't chance the open road any longer today."

Clara gave a stiff nod before she looked at Emily. "Just a reminder. Never turn your back on a snake."

CHAPTER EIGHT

A FEW HOURS LATER, Emily entered the home of the Baroness Robinson while attempting to keep any malice off her face. Her mother had insisted upon impeccable manners, and it required every one of Emily's lessons now.

The baroness even looked mean. She peered down her nose at them with her lips pursed. "My great son, finally returned to see his mother." Her gaze raked up and down him, her frown deepening. "You look how I would expect."

Emily glanced over at Jacob and then down at herself, knowing that they'd both slept in their clothes and dashed out of the inn before they'd done any bathing at all.

Jacob, for his part, looked bored at her implied meaning. "As do you."

"I'll call for baths for all of you once introductions have been made." The other woman's nose wrinkled as though the baths couldn't come soon enough, before she cast her gaze to Emily. "And who, pray tell, is this?"

Jacob shifted closer to her as he cleared his throat. "This is Miss Emily Cranston."

The baroness looked her up and down. "A pleasure."

"And you," Emily answered, dipping into the appropriate curtsey.

"And may I just say, I'm very sorry for your loss." She covered her heart with her hand in a dramatic display of emotion.

Emily's stomach clenched in discomfort as her gaze sharpened on the baroness. "You heard about my parents?"

The baroness grimaced, a flicker of some fear or regret in her eyes. "Of course. Such tragic news."

Jacob straightened next to her, a low rumble emitting from deep in his chest. "We left a few days after the funeral. How could you have gotten the news this quickly?"

The baroness's mouth opened and then closed before her chin lifted, her fingers fisting against her chest. "I live in Bradford, not Scotland."

Jacob took a step toward his mother. "Still the news would have likely arrived yesterday or today. You're telling me that you just happened upon it and then remembered it for this chance meeting with Emily?"

Her skin prickled with discomfort as Jacob's words sunk in. It had to be more than a coincidence. She'd noticed the baroness's comment from the first. And he only confirmed Emily's suspicions, but did they both have biases at play?

The countess waved her hand in dismissal, her acid smile back in her face. "They are my contemporaries. Of course, I noticed. Now, I'm sure you're tired and you've stopped here because…" Her brows lifted.

"A difficulty with my carriage," Jacob said without batting an eye. Emily looked down, not wanting to appear guilty.

"Of course," the baroness said smoothly. "In the meantime, I'll request the baths. Emily, I'd be happy to lend you my personal maid to help you with your toilet."

It was Clara who stepped up next to her, her chin jutting up. "I'll see to Emily myself."

The baroness's gaze flicked up and down Clara. "Aren't you looking refreshingly appropriate."

Indignation rose in Emily and she suddenly wished that Clara had her own colorful clothing back on. Clara had every right to be herself.

But she said little as Clara reached for her arm, holding it until they'd made it up the stairs and down a hall.

She continued to hold it as they were shown into a spacious guest room, where a tub already waited.

The door closed behind them, leaving them in the room alone. She turned to Clara then, her breath coming out in one slow steady rush. "What was that?"

"I'll tell you what it isn't. Good intentioned or innocent. Never let her servants anywhere near your things or your person."

"Near my person?" she gasped, her hand coming to the jewels still tucked in her bodice.

"I don't know. I'm rambling." Clara crossed the room and sat on the bed. "But she must be interested in something. In thirty years of knowing that woman, she has never offered her maid to anyone or been so hospitable as she was to you just now. It's got my hackles up."

That same dread filled Emily's stomach, which only intensified when she opened the lid of her trunk.

"Clara!"

"What?" Clara was off the bed and hurry toward Emily.

"My trunk, everything is...nothing is as I left..." She stared blinking at the now rumpled contents that had not been like this just this morning.

"I guess I wasn't rambling after all," Clara murmured, reaching for Emily's arm and beginning to massage her biceps. "I think we should tell Jacob."

"I agree," Emily whispered. "I can undress myself. Go find him if you wouldn't mind."

"Of course," Clara said as she turned and left the room.

Emily quickly undressed, and as she removed her corset she tucked her jewels just under the pillow of the bed, smoothing out the fabric again.

It was likely ridiculous. How would anyone know she had her mother's jewels? Though she did have the paperwork that declared it, in the crate tucked in the seat of Jacob's carriage. She was out of the tub once again, grabbing fresh clothing and yanking on a chemise and stockings. She began lacing a new corset, carefully tucking the precious pieces between the chemise and the corset. She wished for them to be as close as possible now.

A knock at the door made her jump as she reached for the dressing gown and wrapped it about herself before crossing the room. Was it Jacob? Had he come to see the trunk for himself? She pulled open the door, excitement and relief swelling inside her. Those feelings shriveled in an instant when she was faced with Baroness Robinson.

"My lady," Emily said in a rush of air as the woman came striding into the room.

"Miss Cranston," the baroness said as she stopped next to Emily's trunk and glanced inside. "I have to say, by your outward appearance, I expected your trunk to appear neater."

Emily's brows lifted as she stood by the still open door. "As did I."

The baroness only smiled. She scanned the room and then crossed to the bed. "Oh dear, your covers are disheveled as well. Please allow me."

Emily stared, her lips parting. Was the baroness primping her bed? She lifted the slightly crumpled pillow and then pulled the covers first back and then straight.

"What is my mother doing?" Jacob's deep voice rumbled behind her.

"Making my bed?"

"Mother," he said loudly enough that the other spun about, dropping the pillow. "You have servants for that. I know. I pay their salaries."

"Always money with you," the baroness huffed, her hands coming to her hips. "I'm not living like a pauper like you do. It's unbecoming of your station."

"Creditors knocking is unbecoming. What I am doing is fiscally responsible."

The woman harrumphed again as she picked up the pillow and then tossed it on the bed. It landed in the middle and Emily's eyebrows lifted again. Before the countess had touched it, it had the smallest crease from where she'd pulled the jewels back out from under it. Now it was a disheveled mess.

The baroness sailed past them. "Dinner will be served in an hour."

Emily shook her head as the other woman disappeared down the hall. "It's a good thing she has at least a few servants. She's terrible at making beds."

Jacob's laugh echoed down the hall before he snapped the door closed. "I can't deny that." But then his gaze narrowed. "So she searched your trunk and your bed and she tried to have the carriage searched as well when it was brought into the carriage house."

Her father's papers were in that carriage! "What?"

Jacob touched her elbow with a soothing caress. "My driver, fortunately, was with the vehicle and didn't allow any of her staff inside."

"*Your* staff. You should remind them of that before you let them near your trunk."

"*My* staff," he agreed, his expression softening as he moved closer, the heat from his body warming her through the thin robe that covered her partial state of dress.

She shivered, resisting the urge to shift closer. "How did you survive a childhood with that woman?"

"I managed. Now, I simply spend as little time with her as possible. Which is my plan today. We'll leave first thing in the morning."

———

JACOB STARED at his mother across the table as he took a sip of his wine. He'd hardly drank since he'd taken up Emily's care, and he barely did now. He found he actually liked the clarity of thought that accompanied the sobriety.

It was refreshing…

Like everything that surrounded Emily from the warmth in her brown eyes to the dew on her lips, she infused his life with an added depth and light he hadn't experienced in years.

And he be damned if he'd let his mother ruin any part of her.

His hand tightened on the stem of his glass as he gave Clara a subtle nod. She winked back.

He and his aunt had a plan. He'd told Emily to stay in her room and he'd had a tray sent up to her. He didn't know what his mother was up to, but he was going to find out.

Clara sauntered over toward his mother, her glass of red wine dangling precariously in her hand as she swayed a bit. Would his mother notice that Clara hadn't even consumed her first glass or that she'd been absolutely fine two minutes ago?

Stumbling over the lush burgundy carpet, she tripped as she moved, her glass sloshing a bit as wine dripped onto the floor. His mother straightened, frowning at her sister-in-law even as Jacob kept his face expressionless, despite his desire to grin.

Clara should get an award for her ability to act.

She stopped in front of mother, swaying, her gaze unfocused as she murmured. "You and I have never seen eye to ear."

"What?" his mother asked, her nosing wrinkling.

"Eye to eye," Clara clarified with a sloppy jerk of her chin. "But I want you to know that I never..." And then it happened. Clara's wine went tipping out of her glass, spilling all down the front of the baroness's gown.

Jacob arranged his features into a properly shocked expression as though he hadn't put Clara up to the entire ruse. His acting wasn't half bad either.

His mother let out a cry, stepping back as her hands lifted up, and she stared down at her ruined gown. "Clara! You silly fool. Look what you've done!"

"Dear me. Sorry," Clara said sounding completely sincere as she bent over to swipe uselessly at the fabric.

He pulled out his kerchief and stepped up next to his mother, also attempting to dab the spots. She pushed his hands back. "Stop," she gritted out, pulling the fabric away from her body and nearly knocking Clara's face with her hand.

"That might stain," Clara said, not even pretending to be sorry.

His mother glared at his aunt. "Why must you always be so consistently...you?"

It was a fair question to ask anyone, he supposed, then again, perhaps it was a ridiculous one as well.

Clara shrugged. "You bring out the worst in me?"

His mother gave another cry and then began to flounce toward the door. "Dinner will be delayed."

"How long?" Clara asked. "I'm famished."

"An hour at least," the baroness replied. "With any luck, you will have fallen into a drunken stupor by then." And then she was gone, slamming the door behind her.

Clara straightened up. "That was both easy and satisfying."

Jacob quirked a one-sided smile as he patted Clara's upper back. "Really do help yourself to the excellent wine." And then he handed Clara his own, nearly full glass. "I'll be back in forty-five minutes."

Clara gave him a wink. "Have fun."

"Fun is not my aim." His shoulders squared as he prepared himself for the task at hand.

"Right." Clara took a sip of his wine. "In that case, give your mother hell."

"In that I can promise to do my absolute best."

Clara chuckled as she took another sip and then settled into a chair next to the fire. "Your mother has never spared any expense. I shall relish every sip."

Jacob looked around at the house. His mother had had it redecorated when his father had been on his death bed. Granted it had been eight years, but much of the shine still remained. She must have suspected she'd not be allowed the money after he passed. His father had never been good at putting limits on his mother.

He, however, felt no such compulsion. She had a minimal staff here, enough to keep the place up and he'd not sold it out from under her. She had given birth to him....

Still, in moments like this, he was tempted. She was up to something, and he intended to discover what precisely that was. She wasn't the only family member who could go searching.

He made his way down the hall and into the morning room where his mother liked to complete all her correspondence.

He pulled up the cover on her writing desk and began to search through the neat stacks of envelopes.

Nothing unusual jumped out at him and so he opened the first drawer and then a second. When he reached the third, he found an open note sitting atop all the other neatly arranged contents. His brow furrowed before he picked it up and opened it.

The letter was completely innocuous at first. But it was the signed name that had every muscle in his body clenching.

BARROW.

HE WENT BACK and read the note again.

IT IS DONE. *Wait for word.*

LUCIUS BARROW.

WHAT THE EVER-LOVING fuck did that mean? How did Barrow know his mother and what had been done?

Carefully folding the note, he did not place it back in the drawer but instead placed it in his pocket.

Then he searched the rest of the desk before returning to Clara.

The moment he stepped into the room, he took the glass from her hand. "Sorry, Clara. No more tonight."

She scowled at him. "What? Why?"

His jaw clenched as he leaned close. "She's got a very suspicious letter from our new favorite solicitor."

Clara gasped, "No."

"Listen, we'll have dinner. Once everyone in the house is in bed, we're leaving. If we hurry, we can make it to the duke before nightfall tomorrow."

"Those men?"

"It's possible my mother knows them, but hopefully by the time she realizes we're gone..."

Clara nodded. "They were headed in one direction, us in another."

"She hasn't had time to tell them anything but the longer we dally here, the more likely we are to run into them I think."

Clara gave a shiver. "It's a good thing you're my favorite nephew. This is whole new level of trouble. Even for you."

He winced, the comment touching on that open wound of his. He'd never exactly been good. He'd been birthed by the viper, after all. "Do I cause a great deal?"

She rose too, patting his shoulder. "Your trouble is usually the fun kind. You're a good boy, Jacob. Always have been. That's what's so irritating about what she's done to you."

Jacob had never heard his aunt talk like this, and the words shocked him. They echoed some of Emily's in this way that seemed meaningful and significant.

"Well, whatever she has or hasn't done, I'll tell you this, I won't let her hurt Emily."

Clara's brows lifted into two artful arcs. But she said nothing more as she took the glass back from his hand. "I'll sleep while we drive. I'm not letting the wine go to waste."

He let her take it.

Might be nice if Clara fell asleep. It would give him some time with Emily...

CHAPTER NINE

EMILY FOLLOWED Jacob down the back stairs and out the kitchen door, not questioning why they were sneaking out in the middle of the night.

Some deep part of her trusted him. Trusted that he had her best interest at heart and that he'd keep her safe no matter what.

He reached back, grasping her hand and pulling her closer to his side as they approached a waiting carriage.

But she stopped several feet away. "Jacob. That's a different carriage."

"My mother's," he chuckled. "Or as you pointed out, mine."

Her lips parted as she stared at the highly polished vehicle. His was a plain black that had likely cost half of what this carriage cost. "She won't notice?"

"Oh, she will. But by then we'll be halfway to our good friend, the Duke of Wingate. And the men following us won't recognize this carriage."

"That is smart," she gushed, giving him a wide smile. He smiled back and then tugged on her hand, helping her into the vehicle and onto the seat next to a sleeping Clara.

"There is something you should know, however," he whispered

even as the carriage began to move, quietly rolling down the dirt packed road.

"What is it?" Fear skittered through her, but she snapped her spine straight. She wanted to know, and she appreciated Jacob sharing the details with her.

"My mother. She had a letter from Mister Barrow."

She gasped, her eyes growing wide.

He reached into his pocket pulling out a sheet. With trembling hands she took it, and unfolded the paper to read the words, her brows knitting in confusion. "Is it just me or do the pieces not seem to fit?"

"It's not you." He took the note back, returning it to his pocket. "But we're going to find all the pieces and fit them together. You have my word."

Grabbing up her skirts, she pushed off the seat and half stood to shift herself so that she could sit next to him.

For a moment, she wondered what he might do but he instantly moved, making room for her, and placing his arm on the back of the bench behind her.

The moment she settled in, he touched her shoulders, drawing her close. She willingly melted into his embrace, her face tilting up to his. "I have every confidence."

"Emily," his voice held a strain she'd never heard before. "Don't say that. I do not want to disappoint."

She brought her hand to his chest even as her breasts pressed into his side. She wasn't embarrassed, in fact the intimacy felt wonderfully right. "You won't, Jacob." She meant the words. This man had been a shield for her through the worst part of her life. "You've already done so much more than I could ever hope or imagine. I will be forever in your debt."

And while she held no illusion that he'd provide for her distant future, he kept her safe here and now and that mattered to her.

He looked down at her, their breath mingling as his thumb lifted to stroke along her cheek. "Emily," he whispered and then he bent closer, his lips brushing across hers.

Every nerve ending tingled at the light touch. He pressed his mouth close once again, touching his lips against hers.

She'd wanted experience, and in this moment, she was not sorry. This was everything she'd ever imagined a kiss might be and more. A comparison for every future suitor.

Jacob had been clear that man wouldn't be him, but she couldn't bring herself to regret anything as he pressed his mouth close a third time, the intimacy between them only growing thicker as his lips lingered over hers.

They were soft and yet masculine, his mouth guiding hers in how to move, how to touch, until kiss after kiss, their breath, their mouths, their tongues were tangled together. Her fingers threaded into his hair, pulling closer even as his hand slid up her side, his thumb grazing up the underside of her breast and brushing across her nipple.

Emily lost herself in that kiss. She wanted more of all of him. More of the press of his body, his hands, his mouth. The way he smelled, soap and cologne and underneath, a masculine musk that made her ache.

Her fingers slid down his neck, feeling his skin, rougher than hers, under her fingertips as he groaned into her mouth.

"Ah-ah-ahem," Clara coughed from the other side of the bench, causing Emily to start away.

Jacob held her firm, his gaze staying on her for another moment before he looked at his aunt. "Just tossing in her sleep," he whispered.

Emily relaxed. "Thank goodness."

He held her against him still, his palm rubbing small, soothing circles along her back. "Don't worry. Clara is on our side anyhow."

"Our side," she repeated under breath. She liked that they had a side.

"Emily, I have always been on your side just as your brother was on mine when so few people were."

She nodded, understanding. She'd always known this was about Ash and while that reminder hurt the slightest bit after the way they'd just kissed, she reminded herself these were the people she could trust.

And what Jacob was doing now, he was helping her to find not only herself, but a life on which she could build. Safe with her friends, she would find the right suitor, the one who would allow her to be his partner. For a moment, she glanced at Jacob again, hope rising in her chest, but she squashed that feeling back down.

He didn't want to be her future. But she'd help him aid her in the present...

With that in mind, she reached into her dress, under her corset and began pulling out her tiny bundles that were wrapped in her stockings.

His brow furrowed as she dumped the bracelet in his palm first. "That one you've seen already."

"What one?" He closed his palm about it.

"It's the bracelet I was going to give to Clara. To be honest, it likely belongs to the barony. But these..." She began to unwrap the ring, a diamond so large and bright, she'd never seen its equal. "This one I'm certain is mine."

It slipped from the fabric, bouncing into her hand and catching the dim light of the lantern that swung on the side of the carriage. Even in that tiny ray, it sparkled and gleamed.

"Emily," Jacob rumbled. "What the devil..." And then his hand touched hers, covering the ring.

———

JACOB COULD NOT QUITE BELIEVE his eyes.

Before him, in Emily's palm, lay the most brilliant stone he'd ever seen. He could see its size, its shine, even in the dark of night.

"I have the paperwork in the crate," she whispered into the night. "It was my mother's. From her mother, passed down to me."

He blinked, trying to process. This stone alone must be worth a small fortune. But there were more.

Two more bundles that Emily slowly and carefully unwrapped, revealing first a pair of spectacular earrings and then a necklace that might steal one's breath with its splendor. "Emily," even he heard the roughness in his voice as he attempted to process this new information. "These are…"

"Should I have told you sooner?" Her voice came out in a rush. "I only remembered as I was leaving my home and I thought the jewelry might be some assurance of my future. Mister Barrow said I was destitute otherwise and I worried I might need them to support myself."

"How much?" He touched the necklace, tracing the intricate setting that held the stone in place.

"How much what?"

"Are these worth? How much?" He asked, trying to keep his voice even. But the more he learned, the less everything made sense. Emily was an heiress. Surely Mr. Barrow, of all people, was aware of that. But that thought shined some sort of light on their current situation and why people were after them.

"I don't know," Emily said.

And nearly at the same moment, Clara added, "A very, very lot."

"Clara," he growled out, not wanting his aunt to interrupt. He should have known when she coughed, she wasn't actually asleep.

And while he knew Clara loved him, he also knew his aunt wanted him to wed. Preferably an heiress who could then provide an heir.

But he wasn't doing it that way. Even if he ever did marry, which he didn't plan to do ever, he'd not allow someone else to dispel his problems. He was a man who could put real work and effort into solving them himself.

Didn't that prove he was different from his mother and father?

Would that prove that he wasn't as bad as he feared?

"Her secret is safe with me." Clara waved her hand. "A debutante with money. It's not exactly a headliner, anyhow."

"An unprotected heiress would be of interest to some," Jacob growled out. Inwardly, he began connecting some dots. If Barrow had known that Emily had money, would he have tried to scare Jacob away by telling the titled but indebted lord that Emily was poor? It made sense.

"A protected wife would be perfectly safe," Clara purred as she stretched.

Emily shook her head. "I don't—"

"Let's get Emily to safety first. Then we can discuss the future." He knew that Clara had agreed to help him because she hoped that he'd taken an interest in Emily for some very specific reasons. He hated to disappoint but...

"Is that before or after you kiss her again?" Clara asked, causing Emily to gasp.

"Go back to sleep, Clara."

"I will when you do," she returned, narrowing her gaze. "And Emily, darling, put those jewels back in your corset. No wonder Jacob's mother was searching your things. One of those pieces would keep her in fashion for quite some time."

Jacob sat back, surprise rocking through him. Did his mother know Emily was an heiress? That her mother had bequeathed her jewelry?

If Barrow knew and Barrow and his mother were in contact...

"Does she know about the letter?" Emily asked.

"Yes," he answered, giving Clara a meaningful stare.

His aunt nodded in response. "Your mother and Barrow are definitely in league."

He scrubbed his head. "But how? Why? My mother couldn't have known that I'd be with Emily. Bring her to my mother's house..." But his words died out. Of course his mother knew he was best friends with Ashton. And she'd clearly known about Emily's parents.

"The attack." Clara lifted her finger. "Close to her home."

He shook his head. "That's a big leap. She'd have to know we'd be going to Wingate's."

Clara shrugged. "What do you suggest then?"

He didn't know. But they'd teased out Barrow's motivations and his mother's possible involvement. "I think it's time I pay Barrow another visit."

Clara nodded. "I agree."

"I don't," Emily interjected with a huff. "There are nefarious thieves about, and sinister solicitors. I'll not have you get hurt on my account."

He looked over at her, her eyes shining with certainty. He liked naïve Emily. She always made him feel cleaner. But this woman with her chin up and set in firm lines, arguing for his safety, this woman began healing something inside him. Her words made him feel, important...cherished. "It's my job to solve this for you."

"No." She shook her head. "None of it has been your job. But delivering me to a place where I remain safe...that alone is a greater favor then one person should ever ask."

The words that rose to his lips surprised him. He wanted to tell her that she ought to ask for far more than just one quick journey north. She ought to ask him for everything a woman might ask him to give.

And if she did. He thought he just might say that he agreed...

CHAPTER TEN

THE REST of the journey passed in haze of sleep and wakefulness until at the end of the next day, as the sun began to set, the home of the Duke and Duchess Wingate appeared.

Emily, who'd been watching out the window, gasped to see it, knowing, without being told, that this was the home of a duke. "It's a palace," she gushed as she reached for Jacob's hand.

She'd remained next to him on the rear-facing bench, though she'd never say out loud that in addition to making her feel safe, he just made an excellent pillow.

How he could he so hard and yet so comfortable, she couldn't say, but he'd leaned against the far side, allowing her to stretch out along his lean, muscular body, his arms around her to keep her tucked safe against him.

And while relief filled her to know they'd arrived safely at the home of a man who had an army of servants at his disposal, some part of her was disappointed.

She'd enjoyed this time with Jacob. Far more than she ought. With him she'd had some glimpse into what it might be like to be intimate with a man. She now had some bar to judge any future suitors, and she'd learned what desire felt like.

She gave him a sidelong glance, for a moment what it might be like to do more than just rest against him, more than kiss. She remembered his hand on her breast, the feel of his strength. Even the memories made her clothes feel overly tight and she tugged at her skirts, sincerely wishing she might shed a few layers.

What might it feel like to press her skin to Jacob's?

An ache like nothing she'd ever known settled between her thighs, throbbing in her most intimate parts even as the carriage made its way up the drive.

Clara stretched. "Thank the lord. And just to be clear, part of my compensation for making this arduous journey should be that I get to stay here with Emily for a while and enjoy a duke's hospitality."

"I concur," Emily said, leaning over Jacob to look out the other window at the massive estate. Her body pressed across his legs even as his hand settled on the small of her back.

"I'm glad you're both in agreement," Jacob rumbled. "I still intend to return to London post haste and speak with Mister Barrow."

Emily sat up, looking at him, the worry clearly shining through her eyes. "I don't like it."

He cupped her cheek, not seeming to care that Clara sat across from them. "I made you promises, sweetheart. Ones I intend to keep."

How could this man think of himself as anything other than wonderful?

Clara made a small noise in the back of her throat, a little like she was clearing it but much softer.

Emily knew how Jacob's behavior must appear. He touched her with far more intimacy than he ought. But she also knew that he didn't wish to marry and that his allegiance to her was through her brother...which made him think of her as a sister of sorts.

Then again, he had kissed her last night and there had been nothing "brotherly" about that. Her teeth dragged across her lower lip as she gave him a sidelong glance. Had he heard the noise Clara made? Was he thinking anything that she was thinking? That he'd like to feel her skin?

She flushed hot, color surely creeping up her neck and into her cheeks. Was there some part of him that wanted more from her, that thought of her as more than just Ash's little sister? Certainly, his kisses conveyed more...

The carriage rolled to a stop, and they stepped out, the front door flying open as both Aubrey and her husband stepped out, flanked by an army of servants.

Heedless of the many eyes, Emily was swept up in a hug from her best friend, Aubrey's clear blue eyes searching Emily's as her face pinched in concern. "Your letter just arrived. We were preparing to leave. Emily...I'm speechless. I'm so very sorry."

Those words unwound some tight knot inside her and her eyes filled with tears. "Jacob has held me together," she managed to whisper as Aubrey's gaze flicked to Jacob where he and Wingate shook hands and then gave each other a one-armed embrace.

The moment the greetings were done, Jacob came back to her side, not quite touching her but his heat helped her push back the tears.

He studied her profile for a moment before he turned back to Wingate. "It's been a long and arduous journey, Nick. There is much you should know."

Wingate gave a quick nod as he gestured for everyone to head inside. Discreetly, Jacob's fingers skittered down her spine. She wished she could lean into him, draw from his strength.

Aubrey turned back to look at her, her gaze filled with worry as her blonde hair brushed down one of her shoulders.

Emily gave her a weak smile.

It was so good to see her friend and to be safe, but she knew they were about to answer a great many questions.

Some about her family, but many about Jacob and their journey here. Emily wasn't prepared to discuss any of these things.

"Let me do all the talking," Jacob whispered as if he'd read her thoughts. "What you need now is rest."

She gave an appreciative nod. Much as she wanted to be strong, she was tired and the grief she'd been holding back was bubbling to the surface once again.

She had to confess when she'd insisted he not return to London, she had worried about his safety. But even more than that...

She just wanted him near. And that was a problem, one that was sure to cause even more grief and hurt.

———

EMILY SEEMED to be crumbling now that they'd arrived. Who could blame her?

Despite the circumstances, she'd been incredibly strong. Which wasn't what he'd originally expected from her. He'd expected her to be soft, with all her other sweet traits, but underneath her goodness was a spine made of granite.

It was one more piece of her he admired greatly. But she needed support now and he wanted to wrap her in his embrace and hold her until all the tears he was certain she'd bottled up had been spent.

But he couldn't do that here and so he walked as close as he could. "You're all right. No one will hurt you here."

She gave him a pained look but remained silent as they climbed the stairs, moving past the massive door, and into the grand foyer.

Even Jacob looked up into the bright and soaring ceilings as their footfalls echoed over the marble floor.

They made their way into a sitting room, Jacob taking the seat next to Emily on a settee. Aubrey sat in a chair near the fire, Wingate standing behind her, as Clara slid into the seat opposite the duchess.

His hand naturally slid across the back of the settee, not quite touching Emily but his fingers a whisper away from her back.

"Tell me everything," Nick murmured, his friend's dark eyes fixed on Jacob.

Jacob started, recalling everything he could remember about Barrow and his mother, the jewels, and the attempted robbery.

When he'd finished, silence fell across the room. He looked at Emily, her eyes had drifted closed.

"Where are these jewels?" Nick asked, his gaze shifting from Jacob to Emily and back again.

"Tucked in my corset," Emily answered, speaking for the first time in several minutes.

"And the paperwork?"

"In the crate that was in the carriage," Jacob answered for her.

"Bring it all in," Nick called, several servants materializing to fill the request.

A tea service was also brought in as well as a tray of sandwiches and Jacob leaned closer to Emily's ear. "Eat, sweetheart."

She shook her head. "I don't why I'm struggling today. I was trying to get here and now that we are..."

He understood. He couldn't keep his fingers from brushing her dress in comfort.

Her head dipped as she gave a quick nod and then drew in a shuddering breath.

"We need to get a few details straight," Nick said as the crate was brought in. "Robinson and I can look through all of this paperwork this afternoon."

Jacob looked over at Nick, his friend's features imposing but unreadable. "Sounds good."

"Just so that we're clear. You had your aunt pose as her aunt and lied to a solicitor about the nature of your relationship," Nick asked, his voice hard, his facial expression now perfectly understandable. It was filled with irritation.

"Nick," Aubrey murmured softly to her husband.

"I had to get her here to you." Jacob was not intimidated by his friend, but he did wonder if he'd gone about this all wrong. His compass was not always as true as he wished. And Nick could demand that...

"Don't pretend, Jacob," Clara started. "We all know you ought to marry—"

"Clara," Emily's eyes snapped open her chin notching up. "That's enough."

Clara closed her mouth and for a moment, Jacob was grateful. He'd face the angry duke if he had to, but he preferred not to have the confrontation. But as Emily leaned forward and took a sandwich, taking a small bite, a different thought occurred to him.

Had Emily stopped Clara because she didn't want him? Did she see what everyone else did? That he was no good?

His gut clenched as he rose and crossed to the crate, pulling out the first letter with Emily's name upon it.

He slid out the papers and began reading but his hand, always steady, trembled as he looked at the numbers on the page. Could this be right?

"Nick," he rumbled, meeting his lifelong friend's gaze. "I think we might need the aid of a jeweler."

And then he held out the papers to other man.

CHAPTER ELEVEN

EMILY WASN'T certain what Jacob saw but she abandoned her small finger sandwich to rise and cross the room. Both men stood over the paper grimacing.

Was it bad?

Was the jewelry not worth much?

Was she in trouble?

"Jacob?" she asked, her brow scrunching as the duke turned away, sifting through the crate and pulling out several more sheets. "What is it?"

"Ahem," he said clearing his throat as he held the paper out. It was the documents on the ring. She'd looked at them already.

"What is it?" she asked again.

"Emily," he whispered, looking pained. "That ring that's been riding around tucked in your corset..."

"It's in a stocking," she said a bit defensively.

And then Wingate rumbled with clear accusation. "How do you know what's in her corset?"

Jacob ignored both comments. "It's not just valuable," he said, his face spasming. "It's worth a small fortune. More than my original debt."

"What?" Her fingers felt cold as she looked at the page again, the numbers and words blurring.

"Here," he stepped closer, pointing at the page, "is the ring's estimated value."

She gasped because the number was so large but also, how had she not noticed that the first time she'd looked at this page? Shame filled her. No wonder everyone treated her like a naïve little girl.

"There's more," Wingate called, waving Jacob over. He left her with the page to look at another sheet. After scanning the page, his gaze lifted to hers once again, his green eyes lit with something she didn't recognize but it frightened her.

"Jacob," she let out a strangled cry, feeling strange. The sadness was gone but some sort of numbness was sweeping over her. He was back at her side in a second, his arm wrapping about her.

"It's all right, sweetheart. I promise. Nick is going to take those jewels and tuck them somewhere safe. Then he's going to protect you while I go question Barrow. No one is going to hurt you, you know I will keep you safe."

She leaned into him. "How much are the other pieces worth?"

"You're not just an heiress, you're the heiress of heiresses," Wingate rumbled as both Aubrey and Clara gasped. "Jewels, lands, properties. Your parents have made you rich beyond compare."

Her gaze fluttered open but wide as she attempted to cast them, a greyness clouded the edges. Why was this news as alarming as when she'd thought she was poor? She felt herself falling a moment before Jacob's arms tightened about her, pulling her to his chest. His hand came to cradle her head, his fingers wrapping about the base of her skull. "Shhh," he murmured in her ear. "Nothing has changed. You'll stay here with Nick and Aubrey until Ash can be found. You'll be perfectly safe and then Ash will help you choose a good husband who will manage all the funds."

His reassurances helped clear her head. Her spine, which had turned to jelly, stiffened again as she looked up at Jacob. What she'd always wanted was choice, and a bit of freedom, and perhaps, a real affection between herself and her husband.

She'd gotten scared for a moment but that didn't change her wishes. "Ash may not come back. I think I have to face that fact."

Jacob winced, the truth in his gaze.

"And technically, with as much money as you say I have, I needn't marry at all."

His eyes widened as Clara chuckled from her seat. He ignored his aunt. "But the thieves and Mister Barrow."

She nodded. "You're right. I do need protection just now, since I've left my home and my staff."

She watched something dark flare in his eyes. What had she said to upset him so?

———

JACOB LOOKED DOWN AT HER, choking with his own incompetence. He'd listened to Mr. Barrow and dragged her needlessly from London. She'd be safe in her own home.

Christ, he'd caused her far more harm than good. Wingate would have gone to London and she'd never have been in danger at all.

Why could he never seem to get a thing right? "Emily," his voice was craggy with the emotion he felt, his own uselessness, knowing that he'd let her down.

Her eyes crinkled at the corners as Clara rose from her chair. "If I may, I think everyone might need a bath and a repose. It's been a long, arduous few days."

"Of course." Aubrey rose, crossing to pull the cord by the door. "We can all talk more when everyone has had some rest."

Emily stepped from his arms, following Aubrey from the room.

He hated to watch her go but he had a feeling she'd just discovered what he'd known all along.

He wasn't good enough for her. Never had been. Setting the appraisal aside, he moved to the crate. He might have done everything wrong thus far, but he still planned to help her. The least he could do was find out more about Barrow's plan.

"I..." He raked a hand through his hair, looking at Nick, "I think I erred."

Wingate made a tsking sound. "By taking her from London? You're damn right you did."

His stomach dropped. "I thought she was penniless."

Wingate grimaced. "I heard that part. But the lie you told, you might have to correct that sooner rather than later."

Was Nick saying what he thought the other man was saying? "Marriage?"

"That's right."

"But..." Had his friend not heard Emily? He had and while they might be able to force Emily now, she'd resent him for it later. She'd already noted that he'd failed her. Why would he even want to marry him?

Never mind that he'd been opposed to wedlock for this very reason. He was his mother's son. "She doesn't want me."

"Woo her," Nick glared at him.

Jacob's brows lifted. What did a duke know of wooing? "I don't think—"

"Don't be a fool. You think Aubrey allowed me to marry her without me doing some serious convincing?"

He didn't even know what to say to that. His friend was tall, dark, handsome, and rich as sin. "I'm supposed to believe she hesitated?"

"I have my past. But I helped her solve certain problems in her present. Which is a powerful motivator for a woman. And while I am happy to have Emily here as long as she needs, it would be better for her if she were wed. I know you're her brother's friend, we both are, just as I can see she trusts you. I trust you."

Jacob shook his head. "She did trust me. She just realized that I upended her life for nothing."

"Ask her before you make that assumption," Nick said. "She's smart, even if she can't read a document properly. And she's kind and forgiving. I know Emily well enough to know that."

Wingate might be right on both counts, perhaps he should find some useful information from Barrow first and then he could try and convince Emily of his value.

"One more thing." Nick cracked his knuckles drawing in a deep breath. "I've seen you without her and I see you with her…don't let her go. She's too good for you to give up, my friend. You deserve this."

Was Emily worth making an exception for? Absolutely. Was he worth her time and commitment? That was the real question. He could certainly convince her long enough to marry her, but would his marriage end up like his parents? It was a thought that made him ache all the way down to his marrow.

"I'd like to start back to London immediately. Find out why Barrow lied."

Nick jerked his chin in agreement. "Use force if you have to."

"Keep her safe while I am gone."

"I will," the duke answered. "Eat and bathe before you leave, you'll feel better if you do."

That was likely true. But he had a driving urge to keep the other promise he'd made to Emily. He'd find the pieces for her and help her put together her puzzle. Maybe then, he'd be worthy.

CHAPTER TWELVE

As much as Lucius knew about his client, Tinderwell was still a mystery. He stared into the hard, grey pools of other man's eyes wondering what the merchant was thinking. Smoke from his cheroot crowned his square jaw and hard features only added to the ominous air that always hung about the other man.

"Try to understand, I told him she was penniless so that he'd lose interest. It made sense that an indebted baron would want her for her dowry."

"You are seven times the fool," Tinderwell grit out between clenched teeth, his gaze growing harder. "I've told you several times that Emily is as much the prize as her dowry. Just because he thought he couldn't have one didn't mean he didn't want the other."

Tinderwell frowned, he didn't see her appeal. Then again, he didn't see the appeal of most women. They were so needy, so soft. Nor did he understand Tinderwell's infatuation, considering he already had one woman to please. Baroness Robinson. "You said it yourself, he won't marry her. He won't marry anyone. His mother has confirmed this—"

"Leave Matilda out of it." Tinderwell slapped Barrow's desk so hard, the inkwell fell over, dark ink spilling over its surface.

Barrow quickly reached for it, but ink was already seeping into the wood of the desk. "My lord," his voice bit out, annoyed by the stain. Barrow could admit he'd underestimated Robinson, first that he'd remain interested in Emily after the lie, and second that he'd take the girl and the jewels north to the Duke of Wingate. The man was as powerful as they came. "We'll have to create some sort of ruse to draw her out."

Tinderwell stared at him for several seconds. "And how are we going to do that?"

Barrow licked his lips. He knew this moment was important. His future was on the line. With the money Tinderwell had promised him, he intended to leave England forever, start a new life. "We know that Robinson saved her from thieves, even brought her to his mother to protect her."

A muscle in Tinderwell's jaw ticked. "I'm not sure that was an asset and not a move I anticipated either."

Barrow stilled, the other man wasn't normally so candid. That was good. "Why do you think he stopped to see Matilda then?"

"Either he was desperate, or he truly doesn't care about his mother's claws. Which is a possibility. He's lived with them his entire life. A mother who'd hatch a plot like that against her own son..."

Lucius leaned forward, truly interested. He knew that Tinderwell and Baroness Robinson were lovers, he'd gleaned that much from the beginning. She'd been the one to suggest that Emily would make a good bride for Tinderwell.

Because as much as she likely wanted Tinderwell for herself, both of them were in need of funds.

The man had overleveraged himself in his many business endeavors. But did the baroness know of the fixation Tinderwell had developed for Emily? The plan was that Tinderwell and the baroness share the funds from Emily's dowry once the wedding happened. But in his estimation, Tinderwell was not a man to share with anyone. Not that he'd ask his employer as much. He knew better than that.

Barrow let out the smallest sigh. Curiosity was a devilish creature but one he'd like to satisfy none the less.

Tinderwell leaned forward then, his eyes two dangerous glints of grey in the shadowed room. "She's beautiful beyond compare, or she was, Matilda, and she's got a real mind for plotting but there isn't much that is warm about that woman."

"How did she know her son would try and take Emily?" he asked. He'd been wondering about that detail of late. And much as he shouldn't ask, he couldn't quite keep the question off his lips.

Tinderwell sat back in his chair, a half-smile on his lips. "That's not her plot against her son. That is an unhappy coincidence."

Barrow's eyes widened. "I see." He nodded, realizing there was so much more he didn't know. "What does her plot with the baron involve then?"

Tinderwell shook his head. "It's not for me to share."

"I understand but..." Barrow raised one finger. "I think the way to draw Emily out is to use Baron Robinson as bait. He's saved her, she might come to his rescue."

Tinderwell shook his head, giving Barrow a dark grimace. "She's too fragile for that. You, Barrow, have no understanding of human nature."

His brows drew down into a confused slash. "I beg your pardon?"

But rather than answer, Tinderwell stubbed out his cheroot and then rose up, circling the desk. "You're also not particularly good at your job. You've bungled this entire affair."

He stood, his chin notching up, even as unease settled in his belly. "That isn't true. I successfully negotiated many deals—"

"Any solicitor can do that," Tinderwell said and then, without warning, Tinderwell's large, vice like hands shot out and wrapped about his neck.

The other man was taller, stronger, harder, and his fingers squeezed, cutting off the air to his lungs. Her scratched at the other man's hands, attempting to free himself but Tinderwell was stronger in every way.

"You know too much," Tinderwell growled as spots began to appear in front of Barrow's eyes. "And you're too stupid to do anything useful with all that information."

86

He was sinking. Sinking.

And then the world went black.

THE TRIP back to London was less eventful and somehow more exhausting than the trip north had been.

Jacob hadn't slept properly in days, didn't have Emily tucked into his side while he travelled. Tired and irritable, he arrived in London making his way directly to Barrow's office.

He'd have to clean out his room at Madame Chamberlain's establishment eventually. He couldn't live there. Not anymore.

Which was absurd. He didn't even know how Emily felt about him. They'd only kissed once, but something inside him had shifted.

He didn't want some surface exchange, didn't wish to be on the fringe. He realized that he'd distanced himself from everyone, formed no attachments. He had an excellent outer skin. It deflected nearly any barb, but he'd stopped allowing people close.

And he didn't want to be that man anymore.

Hell, the rest of the world could hang but there was one person that he wanted to bare himself to...Emily.

If she'd have him. He'd prove to her that he was worth her trouble.

With that in mind, he swung down from his horse, tying it to the post outside of Barrow's office.

Jacob's plan was to tell Barrow that he knew he'd lied. And that he knew the solicitor had been in contact with his mother. Jacob would squeeze the truth out of the man one way or the other.

It was early yet, but testing the door, he found it unlocked.

Stepping inside the waiting room, he paused. The air felt...wrong.

Stale. Heavy. He blew out through his nose, pulling a pistol from his waistband. Slowly, he moved deeper into the space, noting that the door to the small office was open. But he didn't even have to step into the room to know what was wrong. From out behind the desk, he saw a pair of legs spread out at odd angles.

His eyes briefly closed as he realized that Mr. Barrow was dead.

The man would provide no answers and a whole lot more problems. He didn't go in any further, didn't look at a single detail.

Instead, he turned about and left, heading straight to Scotland Yard.

It took several hours to finish speaking with constables, and by the time he returned to Emily's home, he was exhausted. But another inspector came to the house to ask him specific details about his cheroots of all things.

He opened his case, holding it out to the investigator. The other man, Inspector Tromley, studied the contents of the case for several seconds before pulled a stud of a cheroot from his pocket, holding it up to Jacob's. "Different," he grunted.

Jacob tried not to roll his eyes. "Explain."

The man stuck the other cheroot back in this pocket. "It was in the tray across the desk. Could be the killer's."

Jacob didn't bother to argue that it could have been from any client the day before.

"Tell me again why you were there at Barrow's office, my lord." Tromley gave him a once over glance.

He sighed. He'd been asked this question three times at least. "My intended is his client. Miss Emily Cranston. He was helping to settle her parent's estate...the viscount and viscountess passed recently." He knew the lie of Emily being his intended was hemming them both in. But this was murder...and he was in the middle of it.

"And were you happy with his services?"

No. Not in the least, but he wasn't very well going to say that. "She'd hardly begun to retain them. I escorted her and her aunt to the country and then came back to learn the details from Mister Barrow. That's when I found him."

The man gave a nod, appearing satisfied. "Of course. My apologies and thank you for your cooperation." The inspector finally rose and after saying his goodbyes, left.

Jacob had shared most of the information he'd learned with the family's butler, needing to explain why he'd returned and why he needed to, once again, go through the baron's intimate papers.

But he hadn't been in the man's office more than a quarter hour when a knock sounded at the door.

The butler appeared. "My lord, a Lord Tinderwell is here."

"Tinderwell?" The name sounded familiar. It tickled at some memory.

"A former suitor of Miss Cranston's," he frowned.

"Tell me more."

"Third son of a marquess, and a merchant." The butler stepped closer into the room. "His interest in Miss Cranston was keen but..." The man looked up at the ceiling.

Jacob rose from his seat. "Go ahead, Michaels. Now isn't the time to hold anything back."

"I don't like the man," the butler said in a rush of air. "He's hard, arrogant and..." The other man stopped. "I'm glad you're here, my lord."

Jacob gave a quick nod. At least someone was. "Thank you."

The butler exited the room and returned minutes later with Lord Tinderwell.

Jacob rose, the hard, scoffing look on the other man's face instantly making Jacob dislike him. This was a man they'd considered marrying to Emily? He'd never allow a man like this to touch her, get anywhere near her.

"Robinson," Tinderwell growled. "We finally meet."

Finally? What the hell did that mean? "A pleasure. I'm sure."

The man came in and sat down without an invitation. "I see you've made yourself at home."

Jacob ignored the barb. "And you. Do you visit often?"

"Not that it's any of your business, but I came to check on Miss Cranston. With her loss..."

"I didn't see you at the funeral."

Hard grey eyes stared back at him. "Where is Emily? I'd like to see her."

Something uncomfortable unfurled inside him, his fingertips tingling. "With her aunt in the country."

"Hmmm," the other man said and then he pulled his cheroot case from his vest pocket, flipping open the lid and pulling a cheroot out. "Is that really true?"

Jacob recognized the size, texture, and color of the wrapping. It was the exact same kind as the one the inspector had just showed him.

His eyes zeroed in on the cheroot and then flicked his gaze back to Tinderwell. "I'll answer your question if you answer one of mine."

"All right." The other man lit the cheroot in the fire then brought it to his lips, inhaling a long drag.

"How long have you known my mother?"

Tinderwell coughed on the smoke and then banging on his chest as he stood. "I beg your pardon."

"You, Barrow, my mother." Jacob said, closing his fingers around his short sword. "How long?"

He didn't really care. The way the man's eyes dilated was confirmation enough.

There was a flash of silver a second before Tinderwell let a knife go, the blade flying through the air. Jacob jerked to the side but not quick enough and the blade sliced into his upper arm.

He ignored the burning pain as he pulled out his short sword and leapt across the desk. Tinderwell was already sprinting toward the door, but Jacob was a much younger man, and he gave Tinderwell a hard shove just as he made it to the opening.

The man stumbled across the hall, crashing into the far wall as Jacob pounced on him. "You'll never touch her," he snarled as he landed a punch right into the man's nose.

"Your mother?" Tinderwell grunted. "I've touched her plenty."

Jacob hit him again, square in the gut, causing the other man to double over. He was older but he was tough, and he was up in a moment, catching Jacob with a right hook that had him seeing stars.

He crashed into the wall, giving his head a shake as he tried to clear it. When he straightened, Tinderwell was gone.

Blood poured down his arm, but he strode toward the front of the house, catching sight of Tinderwell's carriage as the driver snapped the reins. Red and gold, the vehicle flashed in the sun as it pulled away.

Jacob had found the missing piece.

His mother had taken a lover. The same man who'd been courting Emily. He didn't need Tinderwell to confirm the details to know it was true. Barrow had lied to him about Emily being poor to scare him off, and when that hadn't worked, Barrow was now dead and Tinderwell was trying to find Emily.

Jacob knew one thing for certain. He'd die before he let that man touch her. And as for his mother…

She was going to pay.

CHAPTER THIRTEEN

FIVE MISERABLE DAYS had passed since Jacob had left. He hadn't even said goodbye. And while it was wonderful to see Aubrey, Emily found herself crying most of the time. All the grief she'd stored up seemed to now be leaking out of her eyes.

Which, in the last twelve hours, had finally dried up.

It was the loss of her parents, the worry for her brother, but also, and she was best at admitting this in the dark of the night when she lay in her bed, she missed Jacob. Desperately.

The way his hand felt on her back, the way her body fit into his. The way he made her feel breathless and safe all at the same time.

Because of him, she longed for things she'd never wanted before.

Her hands trembled as she sat in the front sitting room, staring out the window. When would he come back?

And what would their relationship be when he did?

Something about him being gone, she'd admitted to herself that she did want to be with him. Despite knowing he didn't want to marry, she allowed herself to acknowledge this wasn't just about learning herself.

He made her feel things no one had before.

He'd saved her time and again, gone out of his way to help her, and somehow, he still treated her like a grown woman, a competent adult, and that mattered to her.

Not that it changed anything if he didn't wish to wed her if he didn't feel the same. That latter part was important.

But he'd been clear that he didn't see his future with any woman. Her heart gave a few sick beats in her chest.

"Emily?" Aubrey's voice called from the door. She turned to her friend, a small but genuine smile gracing her lips as she rose to cross the room to her friend.

"Aubrey," she said as she reached her friend, the two women wrapping each other in a hug.

"It's nice to see you out of your room," Aubrey whispered close to her ear. "I was beginning to worry."

"I just needed some time to grieve," she replied, swallowing down a lump. She'd cried her heart out, but it was time to put those tears aside. She needed to focus on her future.

"I understand." Aubrey gave her another squeeze before she pulled back, looking at Emily. "You've been through so much."

Emily had always admired her friend. Aubrey was one of the strongest people she knew. "I know your circumstances have always worked against you. What I've been through is nothing."

"Stop that," Aubrey held her upper arms, giving them a squeeze. "What you've been through would break many and here you are, standing strong."

Emily shook her head, somehow, more tears shimmering in her eyes. "Not that strong. I'm trying. But without Jacob…"

Aubrey's hands stilled. "He's done a great deal for you."

"He has," Emily whispered. "But he hasn't done those things for me, he did them for Ash."

A small frown creased Aubrey's brow. "Are you certain?"

Emily looked away, staring at the intricate pattern on the wall. "He has said as much."

"Take this from a woman who misread the signals from a man, he doesn't touch you like a man who doesn't care. In fact, he touches you like you're the most precious thing on Earth."

"But…" She let Aubrey go and twisted her hands together. He had kissed her, held her close all those hours in the carriage.

"I told Nick all sorts of things…" Aubrey held Emily's hands in hers. "Because I wasn't ready for the feelings he brought out in me."

Emily looked back at her friend. Aubrey had been involved in her own mystery when Nick had courted her. "Tell me."

"I told him I didn't want to marry, and I'd meant it at the time. I'd worked so hard for independence and my parents hadn't exactly taught me much about what a healthy marriage looked like."

Truer words had never been spoken. Aubrey's parents had never even married. "Jacob's mother is awful."

Aubrey nodded. "I can see why he's taken with you then because I don't know a warmer, kinder person than you."

Emily's throat worked around a lump of emotion, but it wasn't sadness she felt this time. Gratitude filled her words. "Thank you."

"He might need time." Aubrey leaned closer. "But if you really care about him, don't give up just yet. You need him but if I'm not mistaken, he needs you too."

Could that be true? "What would he need me for?"

Aubrey shook her head. "Don't you know, Emily? You're the sort of person who brings out the best in the people around her."

Appreciation swelled in her chest. "You are the best friend."

"No, actually, you are." Aubrey laughed then. "And Lord Robinson would be lucky to have you."

She hoped that was true. Hugging her arms about her middle, she crossed the room once again, looking back out the window. This time, it was less watching and more just thinking.

Should she tell Jacob how she felt? Did she just give him space to breathe?

As her thoughts swirled, a loan horseman appeared on the massive drive that led up to Aubrey and Nick's home. She stopped, staring, her arms dropping to her side.

The rider drew closer and with a strangled cry, she realized that it was Jacob.

"What is it?" Aubrey asked, rushing to her side.

"He's back," she answered and without any further explanation, she lifted her skirts and sprinted out of the room.

She had so much to say, so much she wished to know, but most of all, she just wished to wrap her arms about him and hold her close. Was that still allowed?

She'd find out after she looked into his eyes...

———

JACOB RODE SLOWLY up the drive, every muscle in his body aching. The slash in his arm throbbed, likely because rather than rest and treat the gash, he'd been riding for the last two days. He'd hardly slept, he'd barely eaten.

But he'd needed to come back to Emily.

Touch her, hold her close, and know that she was all right. He'd told himself any number of times that she was fine. And logically, he believed the words. Nick would not allow anything to harm her, she was well protected behind his walls.

But still... He needed to see her for himself, watch out for her.

He knew the real villain now, and the fact that his mother and Tinderwell had teamed up against her...that frightened him half to death.

He'd never allow them to harm her. He understood he was repeating himself, annoyingly so, but it had become like a mantra in his head.

He'd protect Emily from the forces trying to harm her. If nothing else, her innocence should be preserved. What the hell good was all the darkness he'd endured if it didn't use his knowledge to keep her safe?

His eyes drifted closed for a moment, a weight of tiredness pulling at his shoulders, so they slumped down, his chin dipping toward his chest.

By jove, he was tired. Bone-aching exhaustion that wouldn't be cured until he slept for a week. The front door banged open and his chin jerked up.

Emily raced toward him, skirts high in her hands, slender ankles and calves on display as her chest heaved and her eyes sparkled with worry.

The tiredness was instantly forgotten as he swung down from his horse, just in time to catch her up into a hug, her scent wrapping about him as he held her body close to his, lifting her off the ground to hold her even closer.

His arm twinged again, and he stiffened for a moment before he ignored the sensation as he buried his nose into her rich, silky brown strands of hair.

"Jacob," she gasped, pulling back. "What's wrong?"

"Not a thing," he said as he held her to his chest, refusing to let her go. "I've never been better."

"You're jesting," she cried, her eyes scanning him. "You look…" Her gaze travelled lower, over the slice in his coat.

"Dreadful," his friend's voice rumbled from the top of the stairs. "Awful."

Jacob kept his arms about Emily, his gaze meeting Nick's. "It was an eventful few days."

"Did you learn more?"

"A great deal," he said, then his gaze found Emily's again. "There is much to tell you but right this moment, I'm just glad just to see you looking well."

A flush filled her cheeks as she looked away, her mouth pinching a bit. Had she not been well? Concern and the need to protect her welled up inside him. "What's happened?"

"Nothing." She looked at him again, her face softening. "I'm fine. You on the other hand," her gaze slid down to the cut in his jacket, "need tending."

He allowed her to pull him inside and then down to the kitchen where she settled him on a chair in a small room that was lit by nothing but a tiny window near the ceiling.

He looked back at the entrance half expecting his friend to have to followed or the duchess to enter, but as Emily pulled off his coat, untied his cravat, removed his vest, and tugged his shirt over his head, no one came.

The air was cool on his skin as Emily began running her warm hands all over his chest and arms, examining the slice from the knife and several bruises on his torso.

She was the picture of concentration as her brow knit and her lips pressed together, but he could hardly attend his own wounds. His attention was focused on her.

The way a shaft of light highlighted a smattering of faint freckles on her nose that he'd never noticed before.

The gold flecks in her brown eyes, the full plumpness of her bottom lip.

He reached up to run his fingertips over her cheek just wanting to touch the velvety softness of her skin.

Her gaze met his, her eyes crinkling at the corners. "You left without saying goodbye."

Had he? Damn. He'd been out of sorts after their kiss. Hilarious considering the sheer number of women he'd touched in such a fashion.

"I'm sorry, sweetheart. I was worried and in a hurry."

"I was worried," she corrected. "What if you'd been hurt and—" She stopped, holding a hand over her mouth.

He looped his arms about her waist, drawing her close and resting his head on her chest, which was in and of itself delightful. Her arms wrapped about his head and she dropped her cheek against his hair. "I'm sorry I worried you. I wanted to get answers and keep my promises to you."

Her breath caught, he felt it against his ear, the way her lungs hitched. "I'm know you're taking care of my problems for my brother and that's why you didn't feel the need…"

"I did not ride for two days, racing back here like the hounds of hell were nipping at my heels for Ashton's benefit." His hands spread out over her back wanting to touch as much of her as he possibly could. "I was worried about you."

Her lips parted, her gaze locked on his. And then, because he couldn't help himself, he leaned up, taking her lips with his.

The kiss was just a light brush, a small taste, but it wasn't enough. Not even close.

He kissed her again and then a third time, each one deeper than the last, more intimate until their mouths were pressed together so that they shared the same air.

He didn't want to stop. And if he was being honest, this desire was part of what had driven him so hard to return to her side. He didn't feel right unless he was touching her.

"I should bandage your arm," she murmured against his lips.

"My arm is fine," he replied before he began to kiss her again, pulling her down into his lap so that his hard shaft pushed into her backside. "It's my lips that need tending."

That made her laugh, a little giggle that pushed past his lip into his mouth.

He wanted more of her and so, slanting her lips open, he slid his tongue past her lips to really taste her.

CHAPTER FOURTEEN

NEED PULSED through Emily in delicious waves.

Oh, how she'd missed him. The heat of his skin, the feel of his body, the strong cords of his muscles wrapped about her.

He slid a hand up her back, tangling into her hair and unlodging several pins as her tresses fell down her back.

Their mouths and tongues tangled until she could hardly breathe with the want that pulsed through her, and only then did he slide his hand down her neck and over her chest, settling over her breast. He held it in his palm, lightly massaging the flesh and fanning the flames of her desire.

When he moved his hand to her other breast, she arched into the touch, wanting more of everything.

His lips kissed over her jaw and down her neck, following the neckline of her dress, his tongue tasting her skin in the most delicious way. She was so lost, she hardly noticed his hand sliding down her side, following the swell of her hip, and down her leg until it reached the hem of her skirts.

He flipped up the edge, his fingers circling her slender ankle for a moment before his hand skimmed over her stockinged calf.

Her breath caught, the sensation coursing through her, enough to drown her as he made his way up her knee and to the ribbon that held her stocking in place.

Would he stop or would his hand move higher, up her thigh and to her… she gasped to think of him touching her in the most intimate of places.

"Jacob," a voice barked from the hall, deep and angry.

Jacob straightened up, removing his hand from her skirts and pulling the hem over her calf. "Nick."

"I'd like a word."

Despite his wounded arm, he rose up with her in his arms and then lightly set her on her feet. "I'll be right back," he whispered and then started for the door, still shirtless.

The moment the door opened, Wingate began. "I let her tend you out of courtesy to Emily, she's been out of her wits, but you've clearly taken advantage of that courtesy. Even with as much history as we have between us, I can't let you do it."

"I can see how you might think that."

"I don't think, I know. And I also know that you will make your indiscretion right by—"

But Emily couldn't listen to anymore. Rushing out of the room, she inserted herself between the two men, facing the duke. "Nick," she said, lifting her chin as she stared Aubrey's husband in the eye. "Do not do this."

"Emily," he started grimacing. "It is my duty to see to your safety."

"Jacob is your friend." She appreciated that Nick was trying to protect her, but just now, she didn't wish for anyone's interference. She would navigate her feelings and future with Jacob all on her own.

"Yes, but your safety is my primary concern," Nick spoke through clenched teeth.

"Jacob is also seeing to my safety." She gave the duke a meaningful stare, hoping he'd take the hint.

Nick glared over her shoulder. "No, he was taking advantage of your generous nature."

Her shoulders stiffened as her gaze narrowed. "He has put himself in danger time and again."

"Still, it's a breech for him to touch you like that."

She eyes narrowed as irritation swelled in her chest. "It was as much my decision at it was his."

"But he should know better. You are just a—"

"What?" her voice was sharp. "Tell me about how little I am."

Nick's face paled. "I didn't mean it like that."

But she ignored the duke, turning to Jacob. "We're not marrying because we've kissed. Society will be none the wiser and I will not force a match between us."

"Why is that?" Jacob asked searching her face even as he reached for her hand.

"Because," she blew out a breath, "it's not my way."

"It isn't?" But his lips had pulled up into the smallest smile.

"No. I've met your mother and manipulation is the last thing you need."

He grabbed her other hand. "That is very true, and I thank you for noticing."

"And besides. I'll not reward a favor with a trap. I'm sure I can find another suitor."

"Another suitor?" His voice dropped deeper, his fingers tightening on hers.

"That's right. I know you don't want to marry and while I don't wish to be alone, I also don't need to wed right away," her heart twisted at the words as she continued. "But when I do, hopefully Ash will be home or I could rekindle my courtship with Lord Tinderwell."

"Tinderwell?" There was no mistaking the growl. "That man is no friend to you."

A warning bell sounded distantly in her mind, but she was too focused on her anger that these men were making all the decisions for her. "That's right. But regardless, I am strong enough to find a husband without..."

"It matters not. The duke is right. We should wed. I need to protect you from men like—"

The duke was right? Heat filled her cheeks as her anger swelled. Here she was trying to honor his wishes and her own. She wanted choice and say and neither of these men seemed to be listening. "Why aren't you listening to me—"

"Emily. It's not even a choice. We're going to wed."

"Jacob," she made her voice equally hard. "If there is one thing I have come to understand in all of this it's that I have choices." And then she spun back to Nick. "And not even you can force me."

Stepping from between them, she began stomping down the hall, ignoring Jacob's parting words as her skirts swished down the hall. She was done being sad today, she'd officially moved on to angry.

And if they thought she'd be the woman who allowed everyone else to make decisions for her, they were sorely mistaken. She spun again. "My parents never told me a thing. Never allowed me to make a choice. I'll not be in that position again, ever. I thought you understood."

And then she stomped up the stairs.

———

JACOB WATCHED HER GO, his mouth half hanging open. She was glorious when she was angry. Coupled with the fact that she'd been molten in his arms before they'd been interrupted, his body throbbed with desire.

He'd never wanted a woman more. Though that was always true with Emily, regardless of the circumstances.

"Umm," Wingate scrubbed his jaw, also watching Emily walk away. "Until this very moment, I didn't realize how alike Emily and Aubrey actually were."

Jacob cocked an eyebrow. "Did Aubrey refuse your marriage proposal?"

"You didn't propose, if we're being technical, you demanded."

Shite. That was true.

"And yes, she refused me. More than once." Wingate gave him a wicked grin. "Gets the blood pumping, doesn't it?"

The man wasn't wrong about that. "Do you think I can convince her to change her mind?"

"You mean to marry her?"

"Of course I do. What's more, I've got information and I happen to know for a fact that the very man who used to be her suitor, Tinderwell, is the man who is also behind this entire plot."

"Tell me the rest as I clean up that wound. I don't think Emily's coming back to do it."

Jacob returned to the room and sat, explaining all that had happened. The death of Mr. Barrow and then the meeting with Tinderwell that had ended with knives and swords.

"So Barrow lied in order to scare you away."

"For certain," Jacob answered. "But that doesn't explain the note. It's done. What's done?"

Wingate gave a hard grimace. "The question that naturally follows that one is this...was Tinderwell taking an opportunity with Emily's parents being gone or did he create the opportunity?"

Cold dread coursed through Jacob even as Nick wrapped his arm in bandaging. Was it possible? "I know my mother has no money, but I thought Tinderwell was richer than rich. Richer than you."

Nick grimaced. "There is only one way to find out. I know an excellent investigator."

Jacob nodded, relieved. "Good idea."

"And in the meantime, you convince Emily that marriage is in her best interest."

"How do I do that?"

"I'd start with some lines about her beauty, and how you want her so much, you got carried away, but that above all that you respect her."

Jacob cocked a brow. "For a duke, you're rather good at grovelling."

"Aubrey's made certain I've had plenty of practice. Now go. And get on your knees if you have to. It's time we took an offensive position."

Interesting idea. Being on his knees did seem like an excellent offense.

CHAPTER FIFTEEN

EMILY HAD RETURNED to the sitting room where she commenced pacing. She'd been too angry about being told what to do to really process that Jacob had said he would marry her.

It hadn't exactly been a sweepingly romantic proposal, but it had been a proposal. Of sorts. Maybe.

Demanding marriage was something. Had she made a mistake denying him? She hoped not, but it had also felt wrong to just let them decide without asking her opinion.

Her spine straightened. It was wrong.

The door behind her opened then closed again, the lock clicking into place. She looked over her shoulder to find Jacob standing near the door, shirtless.

It would be much easier to stand her ground if he were wearing the proper amount of clothing. His torso was distracting.

Rippling muscles trailed down to a narrow waist, a smattering of hair making her mouth dry. She'd been so focused on his injuries downstairs that she'd failed to take in the view. "Jacob?"

"We need to talk," his voice still held that rough edge as he strode toward her, stopping just in front of her.

"We were talking," she looked away, not that it helped. She could smell him, his normal masculine scent now mixed with the scent of horse and fresh air. "It didn't go so well."

"True. So perhaps I should start over." He took her hand in his. "You are the most wonderful woman I've ever met, and I would be honored if you would consent to be my wife."

She looked at him then, her eyes surely wide with surprise. "Jacob?"

He pulled her close, taking her other hand, his head dropping so that he whispered into her ear. "I can't promise I'll be a good husband. But I can promise to try my damnedest."

"Jacob!" She knew she'd not even answered the question or said anything really, but his words had stolen her air and her thought.

It wasn't exactly a declaration of love but it was a sincere proposal. One that had stated her merits and made promises...

There was only one problem. She appreciated his sincerity, his strength, but the depth of her emotion was so great. And he'd not said a word about love or even affection. "I'm not sure—"

Her words cut off abruptly as he wrapped an arm under her derriere and lifted her, carrying her over to one of the settees in the room. She automatically wrapped her arms about his neck, dropping her forehead to his. "Tell me, sweetheart."

He didn't mean that. Did he? "It's just that you can't spend your life with me because I'm in danger now. That's not fair."

She felt his forehead wrinkle as he lifted his brows. "Fair to who? If you meant me, I can assure you, it's more than fair. I would be lucky to spend my life with a woman like you."

Those words melted much of her reserve away. "Because I'm an heiress?"

He chuckled. "I'm not touching your money, Emily. I'd be lucky because you are beautiful..." He placed her on the settee so that her head rested on one of the arms, her legs stretched out across the cushions. "And honest." He kissed her with a light touch of his lips against hers. "And you bring out parts of me that I'd never thought I'd see again. It's been like finding myself."

That made her gasp, even as he placed another kiss along her jaw. "I've been finding myself too."

He slid his lips down her throat. "I know. And I'll respect that. Take as long as you wish to answer, just know…" And then he kissed along the neckline of her dress, his hands sliding under her to start undoing the tiny row of buttons at the back of the gown. "That I'll be employing all my best techniques to convince you until you agree."

Her bodice slumped forward. Her chest was still covered by her chemise, but when his lips brushed over the clothed nipple, the skin puckered under the light touch, need coursing through her as she cried out.

His answer was to repeat the touch, this time harder, until he sucked the nipples between his lips. "If this is how you convince me," she panted, a throbbing ache of need settling between her thighs. "Then I think I shall have to refuse your offer."

"Refuse?" he growled out, lifting his head, his dark eyes meeting her hooded ones.

But she only nodded. "That's right. I'm going to need a great deal of convincing."

He let out a deep chuckle that, with his chest pressed to her belly, vibrated through her in the most wonderful way. "Convincing…" And then his voice dropped to a whisper. "You are asking a former rake to convince you?"

"Former?" she breathed, her eyes locked on his.

"You're the only one for me."

It wasn't a declaration of love that but that was something. Her insides grew warm and hazy. "Really?"

"And, as I said, as a rake, I have an arsenal of skills at my disposal to convince you."

Oh dear lord…that sounded wickedly wonderful. She was tempted to ask what he meant but he was kissing further down her torso, tugging her dress with him as he went, until the muslin was just a pile on the floor. And then once again his hand was travelling over her calf, circling her need, and climbing her thigh.

And when the pad of his thumb brushed along the slit of her

womanhood, she knew that turning down a rake had been a very, very good idea.

———

JACOB BRUSHED his fingers along her delicate flesh again, the scent of her arousal only making his own need sharper.

He wanted to taste her.

Watch her climax as she cried his name.

But first, he slid his fingers through her slick folds again, pulling them apart to reveal her pink flesh, rosy with her need.

She was gorgeous. He couldn't wait to fully undress her and get to look at all of her. But that was not for today. Today was just about showing her how he could worship her if she'd allow him.

He slid his thumb up and down her slit and then settled the pad over the bundle of nerves that had her curling up and crying out. He kissed a trail up her thigh, licking her even as he kept circling with his thumb.

Her hands tangled in his hair pulling him closer as he set a rhythm that had her muscles tightening and her toes curling in just a few minutes. She gasped for breath as she pulled him closer still.

"Jacob," she gasped, and he eased back, her little moan of dissent making it clear that she didn't approve of his slowing.

"I have to ask again, sweetheart. Will you marry me?"

She lifted her head, her unfocused eyes blinking as she looked at him. "You're asking me now?"

"Rake," he rumbled. "I did warn you."

She laughed then, but it quickly turned into a moan as her kissed her again, his tongue swirling about her most sensitive bud. As she tugged him closer, she panted out. "If I say yes, do I get to touch you like this?"

Was she serious? He blinked back his shock. She was a natural student in the art of lovemaking, as if she hadn't been perfect enough. "Absolutely," he rumbled before licking her again, his manhood straining against his breeches even as he increased the pressure.

"Then I accept," she groaned, her thighs trembling a moment before she crested over the wave of her pleasure. Satisfaction roared through him at both her finish and at her agreement. As his wife, he'd be able to care for her always.

He pushed up, tugging at the falls of his breeches. He looked down at Emily, her hair almost completely out of the pins, brown locks falling down to the floor. Her cheeks were flushed, her lips parted, but her eyes were so satiated that he felt another wave of satisfaction. His gaze travelled further down the chemise that was still damp at the nipple and pushed up to her waist. Her stockings were still on, one leg up on the settee, the other dangling down the side and onto the floor.

She looked like a vision of satisfied lust as her gaze wandered over his chest to where he was already peeling down his breeches.

"Nervous?" he asked, stilling his movement as her gaze rested on his groin.

"No." She shook her head, pushing up on her elbows. "Curious and excited."

How he wanted this woman. But he'd not take her like that, not today. Instead he shucked down the breeches, taking himself in his own hand. "You don't need to do a thing, sweetheart. Just looking at you..." He tapered off as she pushed up to sitting, her face coming achingly close to his cock.

"Looking?" she laughed, her breath tickling his sensitive skin as a bit of seed leaked from the tip. "You didn't just look."

She was trying to undo him with words alone. It was working. Emily was always more, and this encounter was exactly same. She didn't disappoint and she'd not even touched him yet.

And then she leaned over and kissed the tip, her tongue darting out to taste the bit of fluid collecting at the head.

He groaned, his head tipping back as her tongue swirled about his thick head. "Emily," he encouraged. He ought to tell her that her touch was perfect, that he was already dangerously close to completion, but he was the seasoned rake, and she was the innocent. How could it be happening like this?

But as she wrapped her fingers about his shaft, mimicking his movement, he knew with certainty that she was going to be an apt student.

And she'd agreed to be his wife. This woman who was savoring the head of his cock like she was memorizing his taste belonged to him.

And with complete awareness, he knew that he belonged to her. She was rewriting him, making him a different version of himself.

One who didn't just exist but who really tried to the best man he could be. Her lips slid down his shaft taking more of him in even as his hand snaked back into her hair, cradling her skull.

The new him didn't want to avoid relationships, didn't want to hide. He wanted to live, and laugh, but most of all, he wanted to love. Her.

With startling awareness, he knew that he loved her. That this was the woman that he was meant to be with.

And that was the thought that sent him barreling over the edge of his desire in an orgasm unlike anything he'd ever experienced before.

It didn't just come from his body, it seemed to pull from within his soul.

Emily looked up at him, her large brown eyes holding his even as her swollen lips parted. He cupped her cheek with his other hand, bending down to kiss her as he made another promise.

He'd be the man she deserved.

Despite his debts, his past, and his family. Today was the beginning of the rest of his life with Emily.

His one true love.

CHAPTER SIXTEEN

EMILY TOOK a breath of crisp night air, enjoying the view of Nick and Aubrey's garden. Dinner would be served shortly, and she was all dressed and ready, waiting for everyone else.

She knew that Jacob had spent the afternoon sleeping, attempting to recover from all the travel, and she and Aubrey had decided that a late dinner would be better. He needed time to sleep and to heal.

And she needed a bit of quiet to adjust to the fact that she'd agreed to marry Jacob.

She was beyond excited but a bit nervous too. He'd told her some wonderful words and she'd appreciated every one of them. But none of them had been a declaration of love.

Admiration, yes. Loyalty, certainly. Commitment. And each had filled her heart a bit more. But he'd not told her he loved her, and she had to wonder if she was in love alone.

Her gut twisted as she slid onto a bench near the garden wall. He'd used his rakish charm to convince her to wed. He'd not had to try very hard...

But what charms did she have to garner his love?

She tapped her chin. He seemed to really like her touch. But was that normal? He'd mentioned her warmth, and having met his mother, Emily could see how that might really draw Jacob to her.

But perhaps she could help him too. With his debts or with his reputation? She tapped her chin. All he'd done for her definitely made their bond stronger.

He'd been standing between her and the danger that swirled just beyond these walls, and that fact, in addition to the attraction, had sealed her feelings toward him. Hadn't he spent the last several days ensuring her safety?

He'd told her that he'd learned several facts that he still needed to share, but she'd sent him to bed for the afternoon. He needed to rest and she'd be safe until his nap was done.

She smiled into the growing darkness, relaxing into the knowledge that they'd marry. She'd find a way to win his heart.

A rustle nearby made her stand, and she squinted into the dim light, a figure appearing near the door. She gasped and spun, ready to sprint to the house when a voice stopped her. "Emily."

It was familiar and she stilled, trying to place the deep timber. "Lord Tinderwell?"

"It's me," he replied.

"What are you doing here?" she asked, her stomach twisting, though nothing seemed to make sense. Had he arrived earlier and Aubrey had sent him out? Did she know that Emily was out here?

Would she send a man who wasn't Jacob outside?

"I've come to see you."

"Why?"

"Because," he was moving closer, slowly, confidently. "You had a great loss, and you need support now. And you and I, we nearly wed."

She shook her head. That wasn't true. "I'm sorry, my lord, but you needn't have bothered. While I appreciated your courtship I am—"

"You're not marrying Robinson," Tinderwell rumbled as he stopped just in front of her. Quick as a snake, he reached out and gripped her arm, his fingers squeezing the flesh. "You were always meant to be mine."

The danger that had been stirring in her stomach began to beat with a wild need to flee. She tried to pull away. "Let me go, Lord Tinderwell."

"I don't think so, my fair one."

"Leave," she cried, her voice growing louder. "You're not welcome here."

"Oh, I'm leaving but you are coming with me."

A scream wrenched from her lips as she pulled harder.

That's when she heard Jacob. "Emily?"

"Jacob!" she cried. "Help me."

But Tinderwell spun her about and suddenly a cloth reeking of something foul came over her mouth. She struggled for a moment but her eyes grew heavy and her limbs weak.

"That's it, my beauty. Sleep. When you wake, you will be all mine." She slumped against Lord Tinderwell, the world going black.

———

JACOB'S HEART threatened to beat out of his chest, Emily's scream still ringing in his ears.

He followed the sound until he found the open garden door, blood roaring through him as he saw a man up ahead with a limp body in his arms. He didn't need to ask to know that was Emily.

The man disappeared into the forest and Jacob pushed himself faster. He didn't carry a body, he could surely catch up to whoever had stolen Emily.

The patch of woods was dark as he entered, hardly even moonlight penetrating the thick canopy above.

But he could hear the other man breathing, straining to carry Emily. He pushed faster, nearly tripping on a root but managing to keep his footing as a shadowy figure appeared ahead.

Jacob was gaining on him. His lungs near bursting, he pushed even harder but then stopped suddenly as he entered a small clearing.

In the middle, a single shaft of moonlight illuminated the still figure of Emily. A worry so raw filled his lungs that he struggled breathe.

Without thought, he knelt beside her. "Emily," he cried, looking down at her closed eyes and pale face. Was she breathing? A pain so deep cut through him that he dropped his forehead to hers. "Emily," he said, his voice cracking on her name.

And that's when he felt her breath fan his face. He started away for a moment before his lips crashed down on hers. "Emily," he repeated between kisses. "Come back to me, my love. Come back to me."

Her eyes fluttered open. "Jacob?"

Relief washed through him, making him limp. "Sweetheart."

"It's Tinderwell," she gasped, wrapping an arm about his neck. "He's here."

Jacob should have guessed it was Tinderwell. "You can't trust that man. I'll explain everything…"

"Robinson," Tinderwell's voice echoed though the clearing, cutting off Jacob's words. "It's time to finish what we started the other day."

Wrapping an arm about Emily's waist, he lifted her off the ground, carrying her into the shadows. "You hide, my love."

"Your love?" she asked, kissing him again even as he set her feet down on the ground.

"Always," he returned, drinking in her lovely features one last time before forcing himself to spin away. He couldn't outrun Tinderwell while carrying Emily just as Tinderwell hadn't been able to outrun him.

They could hide together, or Jacob could fight.

He'd never been much for hiding and so the choice seemed clear. It was time to end this saga with Tinderwell once and for all.

CHAPTER SEVENTEEN

EMILY CLUNG to the trunk of a tree as Jacob stepped into the clearing, Tinderwell appearing on the other side.

Her head was clearing but her legs still felt a bit like pudding. Anger welled up inside her to think she'd ever trusted that man. Thought of him as the one who might save her.

Had he said that he and Jacob needed to finish something? Is that what Jacob still needed to tell her? As if he'd heard her thoughts, Jacob began to speak. "You ran out in such a hurry the other day, I hardly got to ask you any questions."

Tinderwell's gaze flicked into the woods directly where she was standing, and she pulled back further behind a tree. "We stopped talking because you were lying when you told me that you'd brought Emily to her aunt."

"Is my mother here?" Jacob asked, drawing a sword from beneath his jacket.

"Do you really think you can keep me from Emily, Robinson? I've had the upperhand from the first."

"If you've the upper hand, then why do I have Emily?"

"A point I mean to correct, momentarily."

"Do you plan to dispatch me the way you did her parents?"

Emily gasped even as Tinderwell's gaze flicked toward her again. Pushing off the trunk, she began to move through the shadows, getting closer to the two men.

"I don't know what you're talking about."

"You didn't orchestrate their deaths so you could gain access to the grieving daughter?"

Tinderwell gave Jacob a smile that was so cold, so malevolent, she knew Jacob's accusation was true. Her heart stuttered in her chest.

Why would he do such a thing? But she knew. The jewels, the money…he had wanted her for her dowry all along.

"Fine. If you don't want to answer that question, how about this one, how long have you and my mother been lovers?"

Emily covered her mouth with her hand to keep from making a sound, but she realized just how much Jacob had discovered when he'd been in London.

So many questions clouded her thoughts, but she pushed them all back as another shape appeared in the woods.

Crouching down, Emily watched a small, slight figure pick her way through the forest, her skirts brushing the ground as she moved.

The baroness. It was confirmed a moment later when the moon appeared from behind a cloud, lighting the other woman's face. A coldness that matched the moonlight made her features appear almost like a mask and Emily inched closer even as Jacob eased a pistol from behind his back.

But Emily only watched him for a moment as she ducked around a bush, staying out of the moonlight.

Another glint caught her gaze and that's when she saw the small derringer in the baroness's hand, the silver catching the cool light.

The baroness leveled the gun, the barrel pointing directly at Jacob's heart.

Emily didn't wait to think, didn't hesitate as she launched herself from behind the bush at the other woman.

The baroness turned toward her, the pistol swinging at Emily a moment before her body hurtled into the older woman's, sending them both crashing to the ground.

The shot blast through the air, a cry filling Emily's ears even as she heard the dull thud of the baroness hitting something hard.

Emily scrambled back, eyes wide, as the gun bounced several feet away. The baroness lay motionless on the ground, a keening cry falling from her lips.

Jacob was at her side in a second, scooping her up in his arms.

"Tinderwell?" she asked, her entire body shaking as he held her tight.

"Dead," he answered, placing a kiss on her forehead. "Thanks to you, my mother shot him instead of me."

She shook her head even as the baroness let out a low moan. Relief made Emily's bones turn to jelly. She knew that the woman had tried to shoot her own son but still...Emily didn't want to be responsible for anyone's death. "I'm fine," she whispered. "It's her you'll need to carry."

Jacob's jaw clenched as he gave his mother a hard stare. "She just tried to kill me."

Emily reached for his cheek then. "I know. But you're so much more than she is."

He looked down at her then, his eyes crinkling at the corners. "You really think that?"

"I know that," she answered, kissing him then. "You are the best man I've ever met. Which is why, even though she's the wickedest of mothers, you are going to give her enough care to see that she lives long enough to enjoy prison."

He kissed her then, long and lingering and full of passion. "You saved my life tonight, Em."

"You saved mine first. More than once." She kissed him back.

"Yes, but you were braver than I ever imagined."

Had she been? That made her smile. "I've always wanted to be brave." What she really wanted was to be the creator of her own circumstance. And here she was. Marrying the man of her heart after besting two villains.

"And a wife. Do you still want to be that?"

"Your wife?" she asked with a smile. "With all my heart."

He kissed her one last time before setting her down and crossing to his mother, scooping her up.

Emily followed behind him after she'd retrieved the woman's pistol from the ground. It was finally over.

———

JACOB LET OUT a long breath of air. It was good that he'd slept several hours that afternoon, he'd needed that energy for tonight.

Though he could kick himself for not telling Emily about Tinderwell right away. He should have. He'd not withheld it intentionally, they'd just grown distracted and... He raked a hand through his hair before opening the door to his room.

Making Emily his had seemed more important than anything else. He could admit that. He closed the door again, remembering how Emily had fought for him today, saved him. He didn't deserve her, he was certain of that ,but he'd do his utmost to worship her if she'd still have him.

He wouldn't blame her if she didn't.

He'd nearly allowed her to be hurt tonight and worst of all, she'd seen the darkest part of him up close and personal. His own mother had attempted to murder him.

What did that say about him that she'd willingly destroy her own son?

"Jacob?"

His head snapped up and that was when he saw Emily sitting on his bed, a night rail floating about her body. "Sweetheart, you should be in bed."

"I am in bed," she said with a laugh as she reached out a hand to him. "Come join me."

He paused, looking at her propped up on his pillows, her ankles crossed and her bare feet poking out from the bottom of her gown.

He'd like to touch every inch of her, map her body with his hands. But she needed to carefully consider before they went any further. "Em. I'm not sure that's a good idea."

"Why not?"

"Because," he said as he blew out a rough breath. "You saw the darkness that surrounds my life tonight. Do you really want to touch that? Be part of it?"

Her answer was to raise both arms up to him, beckoning him closer. This time he moved, drawn to her and unable to stay away.

Sitting on the edge of the bed, he pressed his torso to hers, letting her arms wrap about him. "She isn't you, Jacob. And somehow, despite being raised by her, you're still a wonderfully strong and caring man. She doesn't define you and don't let yourself think that she does."

His eyes squeezed shut as he buried his face into the crick of Emily's neck. How had she known those were the words he needed to hear? "I worry that she does. That she lives in me. That—"

Her lips danced across his forehead. "What I see is a man who is fiercely loyal to his friends and the people he cares about. Who works hard and requires very little for himself. Do you see those things in yourself too?"

He lifted his head then to look in her eyes. Her words were like a balm and as their gazes locked, she gave him a gentle smile, the sort that tugged at his heart. Her eyes were soft and warm and her hands skimming over his back and then up his neck to hold his face were achingly gentle.

"Emily," his voice was rough with emotion as he leaned in to gently kiss her. "I love you, sweetheart."

She gasped in a breath even as he pressed his mouth to hers. But as he pulled back, she looked at him again. "I love you, too. So much."

Emily had seen his most twisted and dark place and her response was to confess her love? "You still want to marry me?"

"Of course," she whispered, her fingers gliding over his scalp. "No other man would do."

That made him smile. One corner of his mouth lifted as he sat up again. To say that no other woman would do was an understatement. He'd rewritten every rule since meeting Emily, which was why he moved to the end of the bed, taking one of her feet in his lap.

Even her feet were pretty. Soft, lovely skin, straight bones, adorable toes. He held first one and then the other in his hand, gently massaging the pads of her feet, between his hands. Her feet seemed small in comparison to his hands as he held them, letting his fingers drift higher to her ankles and then her calves.

By the time he'd reached her thighs, pushing the hem of her night rail up, she was breathing heavily, her eyes half closed, her chest rapidly rising and falling.

He leaned down, placing a kiss on the inside of her knee. "Tonight, I'm going to worship you, love, as the goddess you are."

She gave a breathy giggle. "Hardly. I am most definitely not of another world."

He kissed higher along her thigh. "A princess then?"

He could smell her arousal, his own body responding to her heat and the silk of her skin.

"I don't..." But her words died as he reached her apex, sliding his tongue along her seam.

He knew that she'd made a choice tonight. She could have rejected him, found him unworthy. Emily could have any man of her choice.

But she'd chosen him.

He would worship her in kind. Skimming her night rail up to her waist, he traced her hips with his hands even as he swirled over her most sensitive bud, making her gasp. She raked her hands through his hair, tugging him closer. One of her legs wrapped about his back, her heel digging into his skin, and he growled out his satisfaction.

Her pleasure was his pleasure. He could spend days worshipping her like this. But as he inserted first one finger and then a second into her channel, he felt her clamp around him, her hands growing frantic in his hair.

He increased the pressure with his tongue, feeling her explode against him, her body spasming with her pleasure.

He was off the bed in a second, shedding his own clothes before he reached down to her night rail, pulling her up and sending the fabric floating through the air to land in a heap on the floor.

She lifted her arms to him again, and this time, there was no hesitation. He fell into her embrace, their mouths, chest, hips coming together. "I've never needed someone the way I do you, Emily. It takes my breath."

"I need you too," she whispered against his lips. "You've made me whole again. Better. I'm the woman I wanted to be."

Those words touched him deep inside. The part that didn't quite believe he was good. That he deserved her.

His manhood settled between her thighs, and it naturally began to sink between her folds, pressing into her channel.

She didn't shy away. In fact, her legs wrapped about his, welcoming him deeper into her embrace.

He held her face between his palms, softly kissing her as he slowly sank into her warmth, using every ounce of his control to ease her into the act.

But her lips found his, kissing him with a fierce need as her hands skimmed down his bare back. "Jacob," she murmured against his lips. "I'm all right. Better. We were meant for this moment."

It was the *we* that was his undoing. They were going to face this and everything that came after together.

That was when he pushed the rest of the way inside her. She twinged but continued to kiss him as he gingerly withdrew and then pushed back in.

His body was tight as a bow string even as kept his movement slow and easy. She might wish to be treated as an equal but that didn't mean he couldn't kindly and gently share with her. She deserved honesty and responsibility, but she also was worthy of every ounce of his kindness and generosity. And it was hers. All hers.

It was that thought, the one where he knew he'd give her every good part of himself, that sent him over the edge of his own pleasure.

And long after it was done, he held her close to his chest, her breath evening in sleep even as he held her tight, stroking her hair.

Emily would be his forever.

EPILOGUE

EMILY'S WEDDING day dawned bright and sunny, the warm summer air wafting through her open windows.

A fortnight had passed since she'd agreed to marry Jacob. They'd stayed at Aubrey's and Nick's home, partially because there had been follow-up questions to the death of Lord Tinderwell and partly because it was calm and quiet, giving a chance for her and Nick to get to know one another and heal.

They'd both needed it.

Emily crossed the bed to her window, watching the dew-covered landscape as the sun began to fill the land.

Last night had been the first night she'd slept without Jacob since he'd come back from London.

She'd missed him. Not only had he become her constant pillow, but she missed his heat, his strength, the way his chest rose, the way he made her feel cherished, safe, and also strong. She traced her finger on along the windowsill, knowing that after today, they'd never need sleep apart again.

It was that thought that spurred her into action. She rang for a bath despite the early hour and began to brush her hair.

That was when a soft knock sounded at the door.

She rose, thinking that the maid had been quick. "Come in," she called, thinking that she'd ask for a tray of tea and cakes as well.

But it wasn't a maid who answered but Aubrey who walked in, looking pensive as she twisted her hands together.

"You look more nervous than I feel," Emily said to her friend with a laugh as she began walking toward Aubrey, her hands extended.

But she stopped well short of her friend. Because behind Aubrey, stood another figure. Gaunt, and a bit haunted, a shadow of himself, stood her brother, Ashton.

"Ash?" she cried, her hands flying to her mouth.

"It's me, Em," he said stepping around Aubrey. "I hear I made it just in time for your wedding."

"Ash!" She cried again, tossing her arms about him. He felt thin, almost frail. "What's happened to you? Where have you been?"

"I'm so sorry, Em. I wanted to be here for you, but I was...delayed."

A voice called from the hall. "I'm here too, Emily."

Jacob. She found herself lifting up on her toes to catch a glimpse of him now. Did he know what had happened? He'd tell her...

"It's bad luck," Aubrey cried, pulling her back.

Ash stepped between her and the door, looking down at her. "I heard my old friend has been caring for you in my absence." But Ash didn't exactly sound happy, and his eyes held a skepticism she'd rarely seen before.

Ashton normally believed the best in everyone. "Ash," she whispered, "You're going to have to trust me that I've made the right choice."

His eyes flickered as they looked back toward the hall. "Your dowry?"

"Not to worry." Emily patted her brother's cheek. "The Duke of Wingate—"

"Who is Jacob's friend..."

Her brows lifted. "And yours. And he negotiated on my behalf. I retain all financial control of my funds. I'm sure Nick will review the documents with you this morning if it will put your mind at ease."

Ashton's eyes widened. "Emily. What happened to you...you're so grown up."

She gave him a small smile. "I likely did, which means in this moment, I am far more concerned about what happened to you."

He gave her a small nod. "Let's see you wed first and then I'll tell you everything."

Her smile grew wide, nearly splitting her cheeks. Her brother was here, and he was going to see her married.

It was more than she'd ever dared hope for.

WANT MORE books from this series? The Viscount to Avoid is next up! Keep reading for a sneak peek!

THE VISCOUNT TO AVOID

Tammy Andresen

The bell by the door rang, Fern's head snapping up, pulling her from the page she was reading.

It wasn't her weekly delivery of food because that had been yesterday.

And her sister had made her bimonthly visit, scheduled, she might add, just three days ago. Despite living on the same property, and considering her sister to be her best friend, Fern preferred time to herself. So who...who would ring the bell at her door?

Rather than answer, she crossed to the window, peering out, her long hair streaming out the third-story window as she peered around the curve of the tower to see the locked door below.

At least for the summer, she moved from her sister and her husband's large estate to an outbuilding on the property. This tower had likely been attached to an old monastery, the ruins and foundation of the building still strewn about the lawn. But the tower had remained.

Some repairs had taken place, enough that the stairs were usable and the main living area clean. It was too drafty to stay for the winter, but for the summer…

She'd needed a bit of healing. Time to herself. After living under her stepmother's tyranny and through her father's death, she just wanted to collect herself and perhaps work through some of the anger that remained.

Her brother-in-law, the Earl of Sanbridge, stood at the door, a missive in his hand. Drat. Correspondence rarely meant good news.

Nor did an unannounced visit. "Eric," she waved from her window, hoping that he could deliver the news quickly and without a formal visit. She was in the middle of an excellent chapter.

"Fern," he replied with a smile. "Would you do me the kindness of unlocking to door?"

"Must I?" she asked, knowing she was acting like a petulant child. Eric was the best of men, and a wonderful husband to her sister. What was more, he'd saved both her and Ella from a horrid future and Fern would be forever grateful. She'd just prefer to show her gratitude from a distance.

Eric let out an easy chuckle. "Fern."

"Coming," she sighed, leaving her window and making her way down the winding wooden steps that led to the bolted door. The air grew cooler as she moved lower, a dampness clinging to her skin as she reached the door and turned the heavy lock to yank the door open.

Even the tower didn't want to let anyone in, the door having swollen in it's frame.

But it finally gave and, stepping back, she swept her hand for Eric to enter.

Tall, dark-haired, and extremely handsome, Eric was the dark to her sister Ella's light. She and Fern shared the same blonde hair, same blue eyes.

But where Ella was effervescent and outgoing, Fern was broody and quiet.

Eric closed the door for her and then gestured for her to return up the stairs first. She led the way, breathing easier as she entered her tower room.

Her bed, a simple mattress and rope frame, was pushed against one curved wall, stacks of books next to it for easy access.

A small stove had been installed for cold nights, which doubled as a surface to cook on, and two chairs sat on one side, small enough to fit up the stairs and just right for her.

Eric took one, looking ridiculously large in the slender piece of furniture.

"You're eating well, I see," he said as he attempted to settle into the seat, shifting several times to get comfortable.

"What makes you say that?" she asked, taking the seat next to him.

"You've put on some weight. You and Ella were both so thin before..." he tapered off as Fern remembered how her stepmother would starve them as punishment. It was a reminder of how horrid her life had been, but also of just how much Eric had done for her.

"I suppose I have." She curled into the chair, tucking her feet under her. "I know I have you to thank for that."

He waved his hand, even as he stood, likely abandoning the chair and crossing to the stove. He opened the door and stoked the fire, then set the kettle on the burner above.

Which was so Eric. Ever kind. "I could have made you tea. My apologies for not offering."

He gave her another of his charming smiles. "It's quite all right. I don't fit in that chair and I'd rather be moving, anyway."

Eric was so pleasant, it was easy to forget that he'd likely come here for a purpose. "Tell me, dear brother, to what do I owe the pleasure?"

He laughed again. "We both know you are not pleased to see me."

She shook her head. "I am always pleased to see you. You might be the most likable person in all of England."

"Thank you," he said with a wink, pulling down to mugs from the shelf and placing the tea leaves in the pot for steeping.

"What I am less enamored with is whatever business has brought you here. I'm certain I won't like it."

He shook his head, pouring the hot water from the kettle into the steeping pot. "You're right. You won't."

Her stomach clenched as he fetched the cubes of sugar staring down at the pot as though watching it would make it steep faster.

"Just tell me," she said bringing a hand up to massage her forehead.

"You remember Miss Emily Cranston. She attended Ella and my wedding."

"Of course," Fern said, her hand dropping. She'd like Emily immensely. She'd been so kind. She'd reminded Fern that not every person within the elite class was a conniving witch. Only most of them.

"Her brother has finally returned home," Eric murmured. "And he's coming here to pay his respects."

"Respects?" Fern asked, her spine straightening with suspicion. "For what?"

"I don't rightly know," Eric confirmed. "But as he is a viscount and part of our inner circle of friends, I'd like for you to return to the main house for the duration of his stay."

She grimaced. She didn't want to go to the main house. She was happy here. But Eric had indulged her in nearly every request she'd made since becoming her benefactor and she had no right to refuse his. Still, she tried. "Must I really? I've so many more volumes to read."

"Fern," a touch of sternness crept into his voice. "You can't completely retreat from the world. We're still going to London for the next season and I still expect you to take part."

Eric had this silly notion that they needed to be seen amongst the ton after the way their stepmother had hidden them away. What was even worse was that he'd intimated she ought to allow men to court her. "Eager to marry me off?"

He snorted, giving her a glare. "You know that isn't true. You're welcome to stay with us forever. I'm just not certain that's what would make you happy."

She'd been mean to make the accusation. Eric wanted her to have all the option in the world. The problem was, she didn't want them. She'd be happiest just living in this tower forever.

"Fine. I'll come to the house for his visit. When does he arrive?"

"The day after tomorrow. He'll be here for a week."

Her tongue clicked against the back of her teeth. An entire week of conversation and lawn games, and lengthy boring dinners.

How dreadful.

———

Ash drew in a deep gulp of fresh summer air slowing his horse as he made his way to the Earl of Sanbridge's estate.

He'd been lucky that it hadn't rained in the three days it had taken him to make the trip, though he would have happily gotten soaked rather than ride in a carriage. Couldn't stand the bloody things anymore.

It was one of many changes his life had taken on in recent months. Changes he hoped to correct shortly...

Funny how life moved in tight circles, players drawn together by happenstance and fate.

How odd was it that the very villains who'd held him captive for ten months were related to the earl and his new wife. People that had met Ash's sister, people who would willingly open their home to Ash.

It was very convenient, indeed. Ash swiped a hand through his recently shorn hair, kicking his horse a bit faster.

He'd left over a year ago for a four-month tour of Europe. But just as he'd been about to come home, his tour over, a group of men had attacked him on the docks in France. They'd knocked him out, stuffing a bag over his head, and loading him on a ship. He'd awoken in a tiny closet where he'd barely fit.

And though he hadn't been beaten, hadn't been harmed, he'd gone slowly mad in that tiny space without reprieve.

The first few weeks had been a blur but then… he'd listened, to mark the days, and to collect information. Difficult when one was fed intermittently from a tray stuffed under the crack in the door.

Ash had wondered if he'd ever be let out and then one day, after nearly six months. The door had opened.

He'd immediately been knocked unconscious and then awoken to find himself on the docks of London.

Thin and weak, he'd rushed to his family home only to discover that his parents were dead and his sister gone.

Panic had filled him. Weak from months of barely eating and barely moving, he'd attempted to take a carriage to his sister's side, only to find that he couldn't tolerate it. Instead, he'd climbed on a horse and arrived just in time to watch beautifully Emily wed his childhood best friend.

Which was wonderful, after one got over the shock.

Because as much as he had a viscountcy he needed to learn to run, not having Emily to care for meant that he was free to search out what he most desired…revenge.

And with his mind clear, he'd set down to write all the things he'd heard through the tiny window in his below deck closet.

The name of the ship had been Windswept and its captain, Jack. What was more, for part of the journey, Jack had taken a lover. He'd heard her on deck and below. Her name… Melisandre.

The crew didn't like her. They'd called her Princess and Lady the way most men said curses, with rough hard voices.

But she'd brought them several items, the sale of which had meant they tolerated her. And Jack…

He had plans to wed her. Daughter of an earl… he'd heard murmured.

He didn't know what either of them looked like, but he learned that Melisandre had once been the stepdaughter of the Earl of Sanbridge.

Jack was harder. Likely because Jack wasn't his real name. And then the man had gone and married Melisandre and so both were now protected by a new name that Ashton didn't know how to find.

Lucky for him, he knew people who knew Melisandre and one way or the other, he was going to track the couple down and then Jack would pay.

A looming home rose above the trees, its spires and peaks out of a fairytale as a river wound its way around the property.

It looked idyllic and for the briefest moment, a pang filled his chest to know he was coming here to disrupt that perfection, but then he waved his hand. Nothing was ever as it appeared.

Not even himself…

Want to read more? The Viscount to Avoid can be found on major retailers!

Keep up with all the latest news, sales, freebies, and releases by joining my newsletter!

www.tammyandresen.com

Hugs!

ABOUT THE AUTHOR

Tammy Andresen lives with her husband and three children just outside of Boston, Massachusetts. She grew up on the Seacoast of Maine, where she spent countless days dreaming up stories in blueberry fields and among the scrub pines that line the coast. Her mother loved to spin a yarn and Tammy filled many hours listening to her mother retell the classics. It was inevitable that at the age of eighteen, she headed off to Simmons College, where she studied English literature and education. She never left Massachusetts but some of her heart still resides in Maine and her family visits often.

Find out more about Tammy:
http://www.tammyandresen.com/
https://www.facebook.com/authortammyandresen
https://twitter.com/TammyAndresen
https://www.pinterest.com/tammy_andresen/
https://plus.google.com/+TammyAndresen/

OTHER TITLES BY TAMMY

Lords of Scandal

Duke of Daring

Marquess of Malice

Earl of Exile

Viscount of Vice

Baron of Bad

Earl of Sin

————————

Earl of Gold

Earl of Baxter

Duke of Decandence

Marquess of Menace

Duke of Dishonor

Baron of Blasphemy

Viscount of Vanity

Earl of Infamy

Laird of Longing

————————

Duke of Chance

Marquess of Diamonds

Queen of Hearts

Baron of Clubs

Earl of Spades

King of Thieves

Marquess of Fortune

Too Wicked to Want

How to Reform a Rake

Don't Tell a Duke You Love Him

Meddle in a Marquess's Affairs

Never Trust an Errant Earl

Never Kiss an Earl at Midnight

Make a Viscount Beg

Wicked Lords of London

Earl of Sussex

My Duke's Seduction

My Duke's Deception

My Earl's Entrapment

My Duke's Desire

My Wicked Earl

Brethren of Stone

The Duke's Scottish Lass

Scottish Devil

Wicked Laird

Kilted Sin

Rogue Scot

The Fate of a Highland Rake

A Laird to Love

Christmastide with my Captain

My Enemy, My Earl

Heart of a Highlander

A Scot's Surrender

A Laird's Seduction

Taming the Duke's Heart

Taming a Duke's Reckless Heart

Taming a Duke's Wild Rose

Taming a Laird's Wild Lady

Taming a Rake into a Lord

Taming a Savage Gentleman

Taming a Rogue Earl

Fairfield Fairy Tales

Stealing a Lady's Heart

Hunting for a Lady's Heart

Entrapping a Lord's Love: Coming in February of 2018

American Historical Romance

Lily in Bloom

Midnight Magic

The Golden Rules of Love

Boxsets!!

Taming the Duke's Heart Books 1-3

American Brides

A Laird to Love

Wicked Lords of London

Printed in Great Britain
by Amazon

29494256R00082